I0713385

BIRDS of LORE, [Book 1 in the "of Lore" Series] *Editions Available: Platinum, Gold, Silver, Copper ~ Send Inquiries to Ryan Durney*
Written by: Ryan Durney / **Edited by:** Jessica Grogan, Robin Wertman, Monica Knighton, Jeff & Jessi Blackwell, Cale & Mindy Corbett
Cover Art: Ryan Durney / **Back Cover:** Socar Myles / **Art Direction, & Design:** Ryan Durney / **Opening Poem:** Ryan Durney
Thank you Dr. Edward Lense (Columbus College of Art & Design) for encouraging me to keep writing stories and poetry.
Interior Art Credits:

Audrey Durney: Special End Papers Stamp Design (*Platinum Edition only*), Shang-Shang, Hercinia, Cu Bird

Ryan Durney: [Ryan William Durney] All writing, Cover Art, Free End Papers Design, Title Page, Chapter Heads, Gamayun, Captive Harpy, Manora, Nok Hussadee, Bird Maidens of Himmapan (spread), Sintu Puksee, Wila, Alkonost, Siren, Bluebird of Happiness, Aosaginohi, Sirin, Ho-Ho, Wooden Bird, Berunda / Gandaberunda, Hen that Laid the Golden Egg, 9-Headed Phoenix, Thunderbird, Wonderland Tulgeywood Tree, Pool of Tears, The Tulgeywood, Dodo, Ibong Adarna, Jub Jub Bird, Tipped-In Artist Page ~ Tulgeywood Scene, signed by artists (spread, *Limited Edition only*), Monstrous Crow, Rear Page Designs: Flags & Scrolls

Socar Myles: Sagoon Hayra (Repeated for Back Cover)   **David Jernigan:** Suea Peek

Monica Knighton: Rumors of Pelicans, Rumors of Cormorants   **Wednesday Kirwan:** Xorguinae, Kinnari

Font Credits: "Mythologist's Hand" by Ryan Durney (hand-drawn!), Diamond Gothic by James Fordyce, Some of the capitol letters of the font "Yakap" (by James Paul Fajardo) inspired Mythologist's Hand, Richardson Fancy Block by "AbdulMakesFonts," Carmencita by Listemageren, Agency FB by Morris Fuller Benton and David Berlow, Bullpen by Ray Larabie, Times New Roman by Victor Lardent, Tarantis by unknown
Limited Edition Expertise: Special thanks to Fred Legget for advice on many things to do with Limited Edition features.
Research Help: Audrey Durney, Rowan Hagemann, Lorraine Barrett , Duke Egbert, Gordon Fossum, Manuela Modesto Jernigan, Socar Myles, Dr. Karl Shuker, Jeff Blackwell, Cindy Gaulin, Daniel Hiltbrand, Quenton Maddux, Fred Legget, Monica Knighton & Robin Wertman.
Special Thanks To: Tom & Robin Wertman & Cindy Gaulin for all forms of encouragement great and small, tangible and intangible.
Kickstarter Video Direction & Production: Maria Villanueva / *THANK YOU KICKSTARTER for allowing me to try crowdfunding

PUBLISHED BY: UNKNOWN TOME   Birds of Lore © 2013 Ryan Durney   ISBN-10: 0-9840900-7-5

REVISION 5.5   ISBN-13: 978-0-9840900-7-5

~ *Dedicated to the backers who believed in my vision* ~

Here There-Be Monsters

We hatched you into wrinkled margins,
Sheltered you under compass stars,
We passed your names into the wind,
And let them sail afar.

"Here there be..."
"Here there be..."

We looked for you in dark shadows,
We looked for you in vast oceans,
We looked for you in cave and sky,
We could not find you there.

"Here there be..."
"Here there be..."

We found you in our darkest notions,
We found you in our startling nightmares,
We found you in our fears,
We found you in the mirror.

"Here there be..."
"Here there be..."

Things began to spiral out of cont
clean-off at the shoulder, and knocked
partially flattened to its silver coin over
and amazingly the black revolving Command O
being pulled as if against its own will down
him but as he turned to work with it, the smo
splintered gorge and roared, flapping wings fr
heavy silver quarter slipped away. I saw its sp
spied Dr. Braxton. It spit those stars as a cry

When the beam touched the doctor, he was
and see it coming. If he had been able to stud
possibilities, I lament to think of all his theor
reconfiguration of the same mechanism the E
could it be a true death ray in the simplest sen
by a spiteful artificial intelligence once, never
again? Except that it was repeated a few times
to tumble behind hunks of unfinished black b
my pinky toe had been sheered off so cleanly
was no blood and if there was pain, I couldn't
afraid for Ivy. She had tumbled safely but
the crackling buzz of Berunda's blast cea

CARRYING THAT INFERNAL C

It was true I had been waiting, planning
acrobatics, all while clutching my pet celest
worse for wear. In desperation, I made a chi
Luck to fly forth in mortal combat! As I peer
monster had become entirely a thing of its
a war elephant in its talons, which it loosed
hurt charged over the terrain, obliterating my
effort. I was thrown to the edge of the cliff, wh

Introduction:

In 2012, a worn journal was discovered amidst Victorian scrapbooks in an antique store in Austin, TX.

It was full of bizarre hand-written entries, wherein its author claimed to be able to observe creatures of mythology as if they were real. He recounted each experience in lurid detail, often with more than one observation in a day's time. These voyages were rarely dated, but the years mentioned range from prehistory into eons far beyond.

Though the original date of the journal is inconclusive, this author, known mostly as "The Mythologist," seems to possess an uncanny knowledge of the past, present and future.

The store inventory had no record of this particular journal.

'Deemed an extraordinary find, a handful of artists set out to illustrate his writing.

The first two volumes are centered around birdlike creatures.

(This is Book I)

Observing The Birds Supposed Mythological

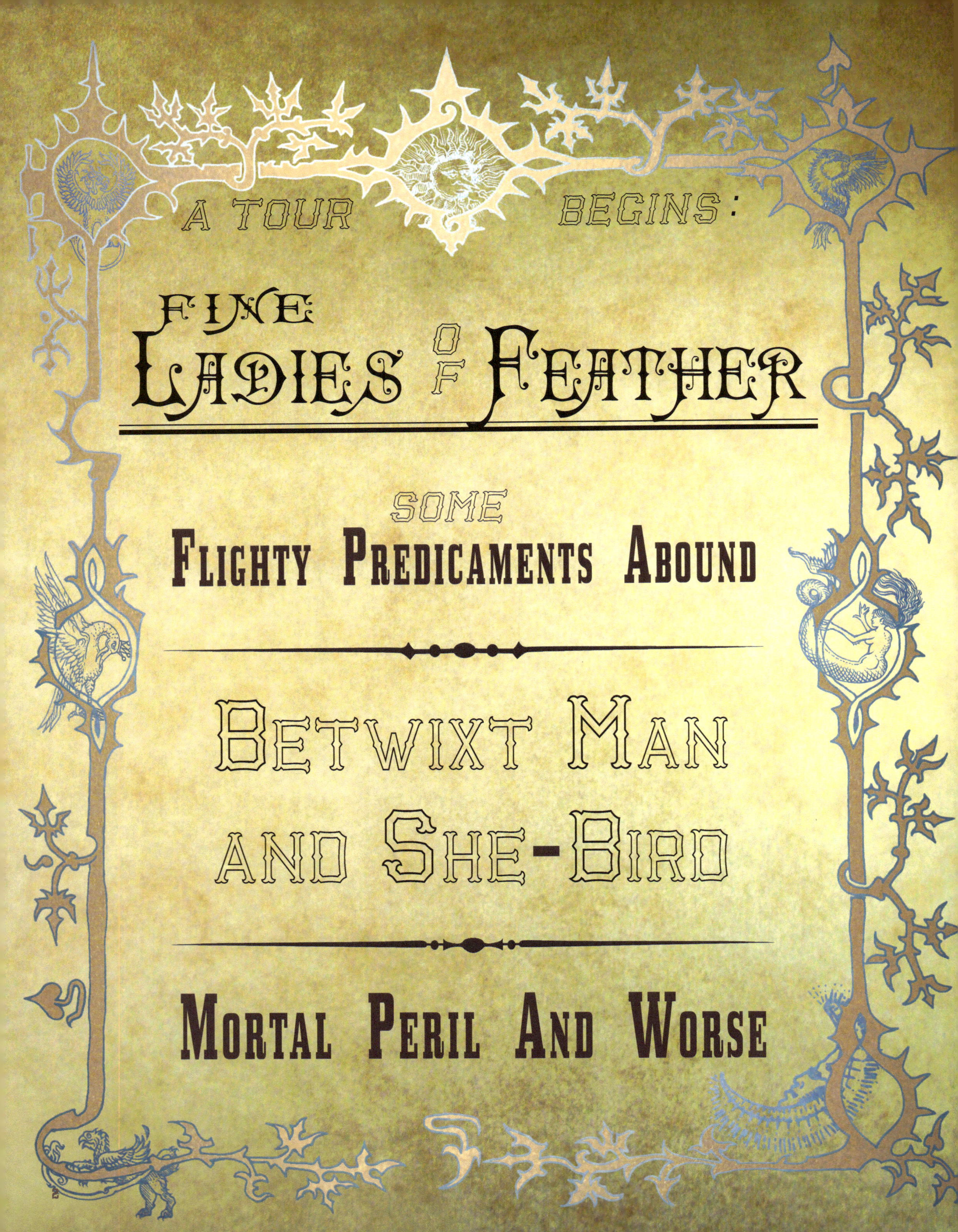

A TOUR BEGINS:

FINE LADIES OF FEATHER

SOME FLIGHTY PREDICAMENTS ABOUND

BETWIXT MAN AND SHE-BIRD

MORTAL PERIL AND WORSE

Gamayun

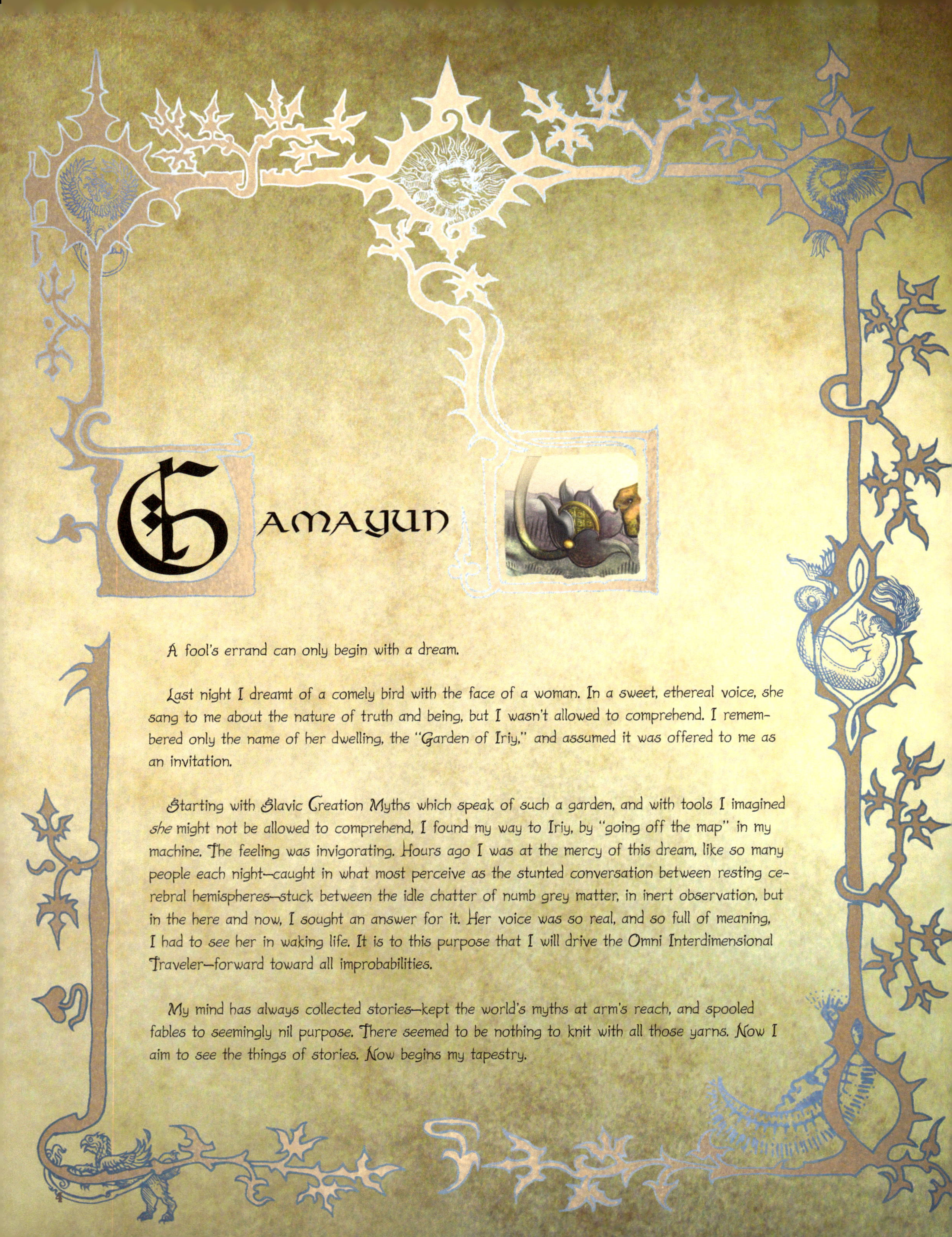

A fool's errand can only begin with a dream.

Last night I dreamt of a comely bird with the face of a woman. In a sweet, ethereal voice, she sang to me about the nature of truth and being, but I wasn't allowed to comprehend. I remembered only the name of her dwelling, the "Garden of Iriy," and assumed it was offered to me as an invitation.

Starting with Slavic Creation Myths which speak of such a garden, and with tools I imagined *she* might not be allowed to comprehend, I found my way to Iriy, by "going off the map" in my machine. The feeling was invigorating. Hours ago I was at the mercy of this dream, like so many people each night—caught in what most perceive as the stunted conversation between resting cerebral hemispheres—stuck between the idle chatter of numb grey matter, in inert observation, but in the here and now, I sought an answer for it. Her voice was so real, and so full of meaning, I had to *see* her in waking life. It is to this purpose that I will drive the Omni Interdimensional Traveler—forward toward all improbabilities.

My mind has always collected stories—kept the world's myths at arm's reach, and spooled fables to seemingly nil purpose. There seemed to be nothing to knit with all those yarns. Now I aim to *see* the things of stories. Now begins my tapestry.

URN BACK MYTHO

With determination, defiance, and technology, I plotted unlikely coordinates and steered a course of travel with instinct instead of raw calculation. Had she shown me the way?

Could it really be this easy? At the helm of my chariot, is there anything that cannot be sought?

Iriy was not Eden, but incredible nonetheless. Every inch worthy of the gilded margins of a medieval manuscript. There was just enough to remind me that I was outside of reality. Every bank of snow was artfully notched. The flora was an improbable knot—more sculpture than plant. The air seemed so crisp and so clean that I felt myself gasping—my body full of earthly pollutions.

In the center of a pasture was a windswept tree. I saw the hybrid form perched upon it, alone in a desert of white, drifting dunes. Somehow I knew she would be there.

Neither of us was all that surprised to see the other. She was huddled against the cold, her long neck tucked beneath her wing. I saw a coy smile and sleepy eyes gazing back at me.

Suddenly at a loss for what to do next, I bowed low. She caressed my cheek ever so lightly, yet I felt the rough skin of a bird's feet and cold, smooth talons. It's possible that she'd never felt a person before...or perhaps she knew I would later doubt the reality of the experience?

"According to the Slavic texts, you are either Alkonost, Gamayun or Sirin. By any account, I am humbled to be in your presence," I said, to break the silence.

She unfurled herself and sat upright, shaking freshly fallen snow off of her shoulders. Iridescent plumage tapered down to smooth skin, the color of winter twilight. Her slight smile never wavered, and I had the funny feeling that it kept me warm, like a miniature sun. She spoke as ethereally as in the dream, but in Russian, which I somehow came to understand almost immediately.

"Of three birds named, I am one. The first is locked inside two songs. The last traded heresy for vanity and was lost. The second I might be."

"Then you are sacred, and all-knowing. How is it that I was allowed to come here and find you, Gamayun?"

"To be sacred is to be alone...You were shown the way here, but chose your own path. I see paths innumerable laid out before you, Mythologist—and some paths that will choose you. What does your world say about me?" she asked, her brow arched hopefully.

"Not enough," I answered. "Only that you are in possession of all knowledge from whence the universe began. That you and your sisters connect the land of the dead to the land of the living, and that you once spoke through the Russian poet, Alexander Blok."

"The first was true until you came here. The second was not so. The third was his interpretation of dreams, as this is yours...Do the Christians still call me archangel?" she asked, dourly.

"And the Buddhists at one time, but...I'm afraid that was all a *long* time ago. But then, you would know all of this, already, no?" I decided to answer her questions with added questions. We seemed to be circling each other.

She studied me for a long moment, all the while donning her implacable, tilted grin, and finally answered, "There is not one fate...only endless reaction. There will be one *you* must teach this to. In dreams I've asked you many questions to which I already know all answers, save for one. Tell me...*what is this worth to you?*"

"You mean, seeing you? Knowing you exist beyond old paintings?...*Everything*," I said, with ease.

"So it will be. And you may lose what you name to gamble," she stated, letting a more dour tone break her cheerful, ethereal nature again, if only for a split second.

Further conversation ensued, that is extremely hard to remember. I do recall, eventually, that I had the sense that I might be, by her presence alone, lulled into infinite conversation. I believe there may be perils in associating too long with her ilk, and I make a note of this now. Such is the nature of deities. It is not beyond possibility that time passes differently in realms such as hers and so I began my grand exit speech:

"While I am indebted to you in so many ways...and I appreciate the magnitude of such an esteemed, unearthly and cosmic counsel, I believe I might be best suited to bid you farewell, wondrous lady. Rest assured, *I* will not forget y-"

"Mythologist," she interrupted, "One leads to another. That is your way from here on out. That is how you'll do it."

She twisted gracefully and managed to unhinge a thin golden chain, dripping with tiny rubies. I noticed for the first time, that she was beset with many jeweled necklaces. There was no time to wonder where she got them. I thanked her many times, even though a gift of jewelry, from a being before time, seemed a very odd thing.

"I will not begin my important work with the same prophetic nonsense of dreams!" is what I thought to myself, as I turned to follow my deep tracks back to my machine. To her, it was as if I had spoken aloud, and I heard her answer from a distance:

"Ahh, but there can be no other way now. You came here...and I am, after all...*only* prophecy."

XORGUINAE

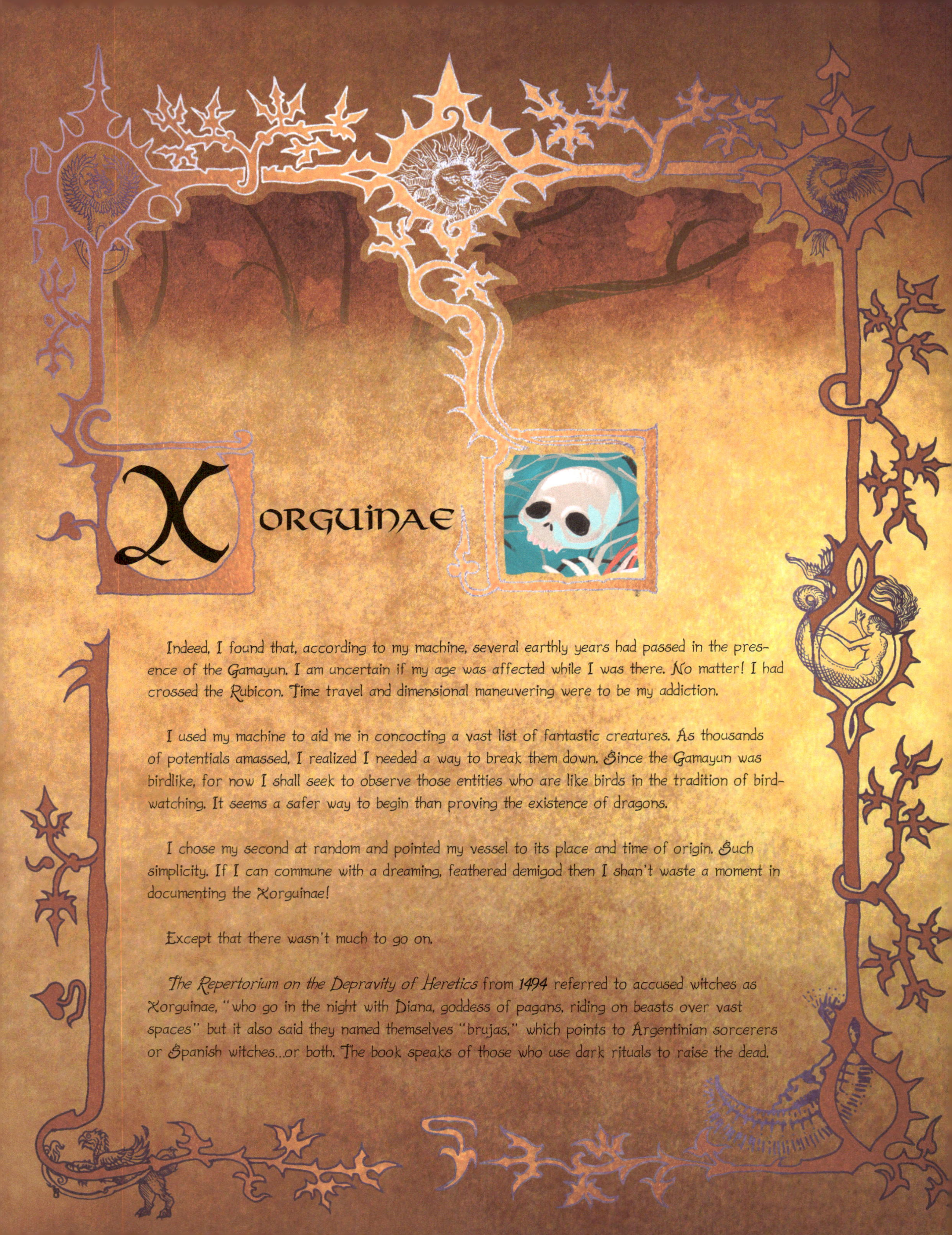

Indeed, I found that, according to my machine, several earthly years had passed in the presence of the Gamayun. I am uncertain if my age was affected while I was there. No matter! I had crossed the Rubicon. Time travel and dimensional maneuvering were to be my addiction.

I used my machine to aid me in concocting a vast list of fantastic creatures. As thousands of potentials amassed, I realized I needed a way to break them down. Since the Gamayun was birdlike, for now I shall seek to observe those entities who are like birds in the tradition of birdwatching. It seems a safer way to begin than proving the existence of dragons.

I chose my second at random and pointed my vessel to its place and time of origin. Such simplicity. If I can commune with a dreaming, feathered demigod then I shan't waste a moment in documenting the Xorguinae!

Except that there wasn't much to go on.

The Repertorium on the Depravity of Heretics from *1494* referred to accused witches as Xorguinae, "who go in the night with Diana, goddess of pagans, riding on beasts over vast spaces" but it also said they named themselves "brujas," which points to Argentinian sorcerers or Spanish witches...or both. The book speaks of those who use dark rituals to raise the dead.

And so I followed cold trails in time to investigate several necromancers, fearing my quarry was leading me some place dark and terrible. Yet all of these infamous men ended up as charlatans or rumors, save for one, who was Portuguese. He wasn't able to raise the dead, but he said the Xorguinae were real, and that he could take me to them for a coin. I had no suitable money for his time or place so I departed and returned with copious amounts of food. This turned out to be equally exciting to this poor, great "necromancer."

We marched deep into what I now believe was the Iberian Peninsula. The forest was silent before dawn, save for dripping mosses and the shedding of spiny chestnut hulls from above. The old man led me off the crumbling road, down deer paths, and into a valley of towering cork oaks. I was concerned he might simply be leading me to where no one would see him bludgeon me to death so he could loot my body in the cold morning dew. As before, this necromancer had no black heart to direct such a crime. He gestured toward two branches hanging over a cliff. His face went white and for the first time I realized that he was afraid of this place. He pointed again and nodded, exclaiming in short breaths, "Xorguinae—*they are not like the witches they hang in the village. I will go no further.*"

I leaned over the slick stone edge. My eyes found a darkened mass. Something had clumped pine brush together with mud and dead grass. My mind spun to imagine the proper bird or mammal for this time and region but there was nothing large enough for the circumference of the nest. My time to ponder was cut short by a calamity behind us. A troop of very small beings were stepping lightly down the edge of the cliff. They were confabulating in the harshest of bird calls, much like the rusty, metallic scrapes of a plague of grackles.

At first they looked like naked children, all female, but where arms might have swayed to their gait, stumpy wings idly flapped. What seemed like messy, short-cropped hair must have been blue-black feathers, contrasting with the skin of their human parts, which was speckled in mud. There was an aspect of menace gleaming in their eerie blue eyes.

My poor necromancer. He tried to scramble up the hill, but they swarmed him and took turns making paralytic bites upon his neck, shoulders, and legs. A murderous throng of vampiric sub-human birds!

There was little intellect and no mercy in the feeding of the Xorguinae fledgelings. They bled him out and let his body thud to the slick stone, stiffened by fear, or exsanguination—all the while keeping one eye on *me.* I'll be haunted by his look of frozen terror as long as I live, and forever regret my ignorance in believing that a tour seeking "monsters" wouldn't find some. I was wrong. It wasn't always going to be exalting. This is what comes of running before I have learned to walk.

They turned to me next, their mouths frothing. There was a pattering of hardened bird feet upon smooth stone. Time stuttered. I remember the light of dawn reaching over us, and its translucent effect of red light on the blood-stained needle-teeth in their gaping mouths. Red upon red. Red in tooth and claw. *Are these things only animals? How can they* be *here? Did I leave the Gamayun's dimension only to return to an alternate earth, where half-human birds are not hard to find? Have I been blessed or cursed? I would never know if I died here, and that bothered me most of all.*

I fumbled in my pockets nonetheless, and pulled out the shining chain of rubies gifted to me by the Gamayun. In the blazing dawn, the jewels threw caustic light upon the stone and the trees. The fledgelings were dazzled by this. The effect was every bit as paralytic to them as their venom had been to the necromancer and I was able to stumble backwards, far enough, that they turned back to feed on their first kill.

I am left with the shame of leading that poor man to die.

My next birding would lead me to an isolated castle in the Mediterranean, where, considering the memories now attached, I gladly traded the ruby necklace as the price of admission. Now I'm left to ponder if I am merely behaving in tow with what the Gamayun said? Is all of this self-fulfilling?

*Note: I now have a vested curiosity as to what a vampire truly *is*..but that is another tour for another day.

HARPY

The following is a transcript, to the best of my memory, between myself and who I deemed to be, quite possibly the last living harpy:

"Lady Ocypete, you are even more beautiful than I'd heard," I said.

I bowed low, and a smile crept to the corners of her delicate lips, but only for a moment. She offered her hand to be kissed, which I did, gladly. Her skin was soft and perfumed in jasmine.

"They'd warned me that you could be charming," she said, turning her gaze upon the vast ocean vista that her balcony afforded.

"I am merely awe-sticken by the presence of royalty. Is it true that you were named after your great, great, great grandmother, Ocypete, the Queen of your kind? Ocypete the cruel, Ocypete Swiftwind, who they say, sewed discord for Zeus himself?" I posed, hoping for a trifle on the true origin of harpies.

"Yes, well, I can see the lady and lord spared you no respite before reciting their favorite yarn, for their favorite living treasure. Every time I am presented as the rare collectible curiosity that I am, they roll out a velvet carpet and carry me in a litter, as the onlookers gasp, wide-eyed. You can't blame me for wondering if that part of the tale, about my grand and wondrous ancestry is only another facet of the farce?" she answered, rolling her eyes.

"I admit that you are a wonder to behold, but there is nothing about you that is farce, despite what tales they adorn you with. Even without your more...unique qualities, you should be counted as one of the most beautiful women I have ever known," I tried, meaning to lift her spirits again.

Here, I made the mistake of letting my eyes linger on her bird's legs. They were somewhere between those of an ostrich and a powerful bird of prey. She did her best to hide them, as special silken wraps had been woven around her ankles and jewelry dripped between her toes.

She looked down, and shuffled her feet on the stool. She even tried to cover her legs with her skirt a bit more, but her flowing tail got in the way. It was then that I noticed how much of a burden it seemed to be to carry that heavy tail, and also...that the tail itself was of mismatched plumage.

Finally, she broke the silence saying, "More than half of me is already adornment. Do you see this tail? It's pinned to the dress. By the time I am aged, I fear that there will be nothing left of me but adornment. I have nightmares of being stuffed alive, and hung in the parlor."

I thought of how woeful and lonely she seemed perched by her balcony, ever-staring out across the Ionian Sea toward the Seven Islands of Greece. There were many empty flagons of wine. The fanciful gifts and morsels that were heaped upon her went mostly untouched. I joined her at the balcony and listened to the waves crash far below.

Finally I broke the silence in a gentle tone...wondering aloud, "If...you did find them...huddled in some cave in Minoa...or a ledge along the coast of Strophades...what would you do? Degenerate to the savagery of your harpy sisters? Join them in their piracy and carnage? Starve naked, alongside them, in the cold, and the rain, with the blood of sailors on your talons?"

"*Please...Enough*," she said, flatly. "Don't you think I understand that I am condemned?"

Another long, gloomy silence...she staring ever-skyward. I hung my head, but couldn't bear not telling her, "I checked, dear lady...there are none left there, to storm this palace, and snatch their princess back. I'm sad to say your fears are well-founded."

As a final glum observation, I noted that they had clipped every other feather from the tips of her wings, to keep her forever bound here, under the illusion of freedom.

Her parting words now haunt me, "But you are wrong, Mythologist...All I have ever wanted...was to fly."

I left her balcony heavy-hearted, and we said nothing more to one another. Her "family" tried their best to up-raise my encounter. I could see in their eyes that many a spectator had left similarly downtrodden. The realization that I had come to stare, like all the rest, made me even more glum. Was I nothing more than an interchronological zoo-goer, whose only purpose was to gawk?

Seeing as how I entered under the guise of a royal bard of elsewhere, the courtiers plied me with small treasures. This gave me an idea for a voyage, and I accepted several, but only if they also gifted me a jar of equal splendor, to collect them in.

Kinnari

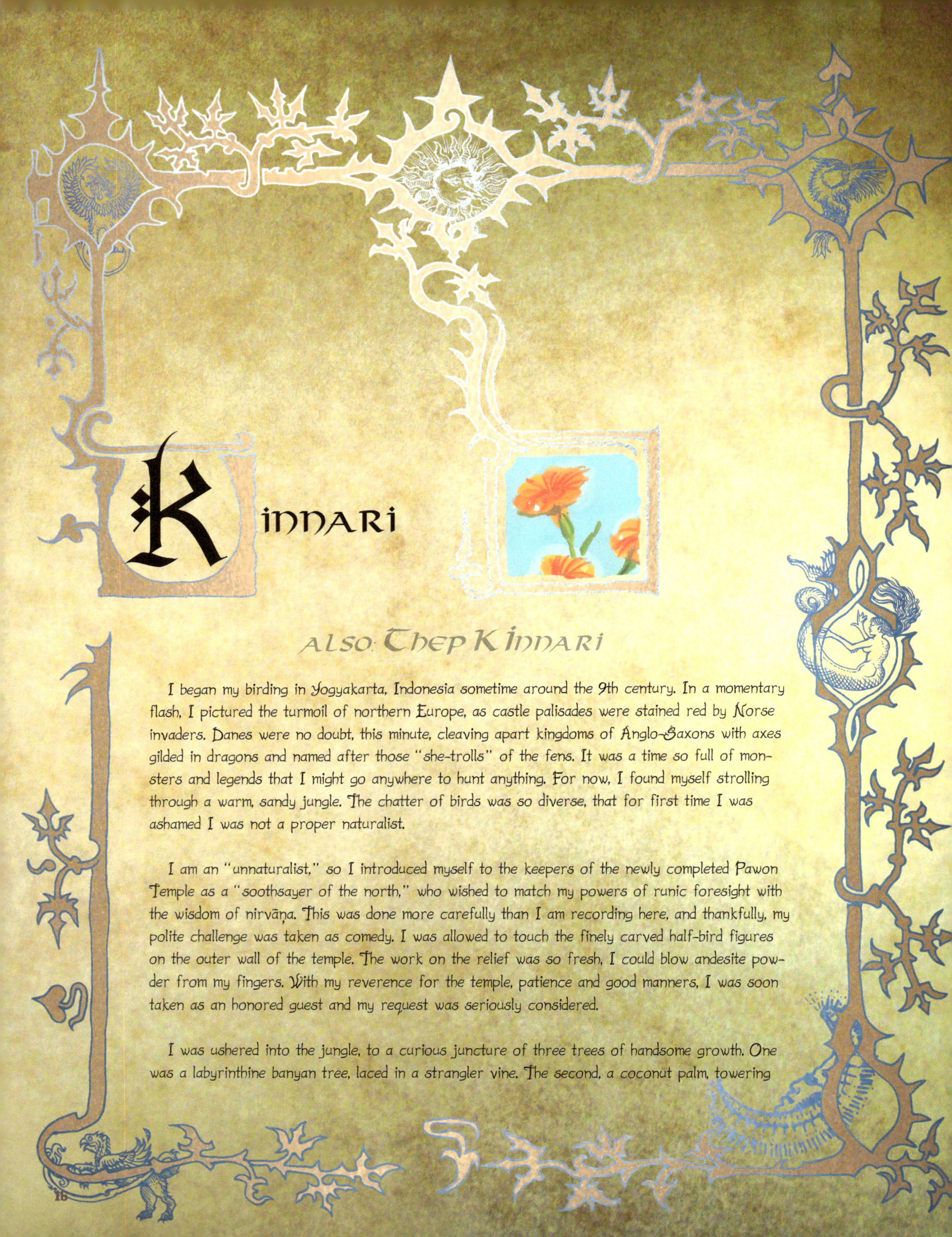

I began my birding in Yogyakarta, Indonesia sometime around the 9th century. In a momentary flash, I pictured the turmoil of northern Europe, as castle palisades were stained red by Norse invaders. Danes were no doubt, this minute, cleaving apart kingdoms of Anglo-Saxons with axes gilded in dragons and named after those "she-trolls" of the fens. It was a time so full of monsters and legends that I might go anywhere to hunt anything. For now, I found myself strolling through a warm, sandy jungle. The chatter of birds was so diverse, that for first time I was ashamed I was not a proper naturalist.

I am an "unnaturalist," so I introduced myself to the keepers of the newly completed Pawon Temple as a "soothsayer of the north," who wished to match my powers of runic foresight with the wisdom of nirvāṇa. This was done more carefully than I am recording here, and thankfully, my polite challenge was taken as comedy. I was allowed to touch the finely carved half-bird figures on the outer wall of the temple. The work on the relief was so fresh, I could blow andesite powder from my fingers. With my reverence for the temple, patience and good manners, I was soon taken as an honored guest and my request was seriously considered.

I was ushered into the jungle, to a curious juncture of three trees of handsome growth. One was a labyrinthine banyan tree, laced in a strangler vine. The second, a coconut palm, towering

and loaded with fruit. The last, a baobab that shamed the others with its elephantine girth and sky-scraping umbrella canopy. I was to choose which tree was the true Kalpataru, or the divine "Tree of Life." If I chose truly, it would "grant my innermost desire."

Since to them, I was a mystic of sorts, I was trusted to be alone in my soothsaying in this sacred spot. The moment they departed, I admit I went about it with the villainy of the futurist. Shedding mysticism for the cold calculations of my machine, I found the trace particles of a portal to an echo dimension, and punctured through all three trees at once.

Despite beginning in Indonesia, I was teleported somewhere into the base circumference of the Himalayan mountains. I had taken advantage of the strong beliefs of the fresh temple's devotees and jettisoned through the rift that their imaginings had left slightly ajar. As confirmed by the Omni's detection systems, I was in a place that had no true time nor earthly geography—a place that could be no "place" at all. The ear marks of another dimension. I had hoped to have found the sacred garden that held live versions of the kinnari and kinnara statues.

The other jungle that awaited me was of immediate otherworldly magnitude. Before I could take it in, I was beset by a guardian of sorts, perched on the branches of what was now only the solitary banyan tree. She was far more amazing than her relief carving. Her feather palette was that of a Military Macaw, yet with a metallic sheen to match the gold and jewels that adorned her. She spoke in echoing Old Malay, which I quickly understood.

"Is it the Kinnari, then...said to guard the Tree of Life?" I asked, to get the ball rolling.

"That, and more, but the least of the visions you might take from this grove of Himmapan," was her answer.

"Never! You are without equal, and no amount of jewelry could outshine your emerald eyes," I replied, and this was not mere flattery, but flattery with the dual purpose of self-preservation.

There was something cunning about the piercing gleam in her eyes that gave me pause. The charm of a wayward mortal wasn't going to get me all that far. I made what I hoped would be the first of several low bows that day. Her expression softened. So far, there was something of an advantage to being a mortal observer of celestial beings. My acknowledgement alone seemed like some sort of currency.

She never broke her piercing stare. Finally, I said, nervously, "I see no jar of treasure upon your branch. Allow me to present your first."

I held it aloft, and this was taken with surprising eagerness. In a blurred swoop the heavy jar was snatched away. It was clear that no matter how pretty my words, gold would outshine them in value.

"If you have only come here to pay tribute to the beauty of this place, you might be allowed passage," she permitted. "But save your flattery for there are those here who will devour your attentions. I accept your token of passage, but...do you understand that each sight in Himmapan may demand its *own* tribute?"

"I accept. I am here to see...not despoil," I said earnestly.

The Kinnari nodded, and with the same careful, judging look, stated, "May you learn they are the same...Tell me, though, you see me now upon this banyan, but...which tree would you have chosen as the portal? Answer truly, this time, Mythologist."

I thought for a moment, and reached for an answer that might please her, and show my wisdom, but instead began to run at the mouth, saying, "My instinct was with the grandest—the baobab. 'Just look at your forest! But, then...perhaps the fecundity of the coconut tree might have been the better answer? As the world overpopulates in the mid 2000's, it's coconuts and palm oil that save Indon-"

I was interrupted by Kinnari laughter, which was like the tinkling of bells, in staggered chorus—not unpleasant, but so unlike any human voice, or bird noise, that I was jarred by it. Then she said, "It was never about nirvana. The test was to choose *your* Tree of Life. Look upon my perch and know all there is to know."

I looked hard at the banyan, and wondered if there was something metaphorical in the strangling vine that enveloped it. I am thinking of it now, as I write this, but I am still not sure of her lesson. I can only hope that the ignorance of mortals is also currency in celestial places...(but I think I know better).

Thinking of her swift talons and wishing to escape her penetrating gaze, I tried, "Then...might I take a short walk through this garden forest, Kinnari?"

"You are granted the enlightenment of this grove because you are as much a wonder here, as it is unto you... That, and Indra finds you amusing. You are to be the first, and the last, Mythologist. Remember, there is a fine line between explorer and transgressor."

Bird Maidens of Himmapan

Manora & the

I found my way to a path of sorts. I was afraid of marking the magnificent flora in symbols of navigation, in case it would be taken as graffiti—or worse, an incantation from the future. Her words had left me distracted from the sights and sounds of Himmapan, so I stopped to gather myself. Instead, I was horrified! Ahead, over a knoll, were what I perceived to be the dangling bodies of dead women, brutally hung by their hair. I rushed to the scene in blind anguish but I couldn't have been more wrong.

The hung women were the growing fruits of a Nariphon Tree! I paced around them in wonder, tracing their growth cycle from the top of the tree to the bottom. All began as pods upon vinelike branches—some of which are ground-creeping, so as to aid in bearing the weight. The pods slowly turn inside-out, at which point all but their "spine" and the backs of their heads, are fully formed. By human standards, they already appear to be aged to nearly twenty years when the pod begins to peel back. The higher-up, less ripened forms are not so much infantile as miniature in shape, giving the crown the strange appearance of a Christmas tree ornamented in sleeping, fairy vegetables. The entire crown of growing girlish pods seemed as inanimate as any other tree's...at first.

The tree must have been aware of my presence, and perhaps attempted to fulfill a function in its life cycle, which involved myself and several seed maidens, who had dislodged quietly from their

stems to surround me. The fully formed beings were of a curious singular purpose, armed with unnatural beauty, whose only "flaw" was a heightened green translucence in bright sun. They possessed a glint of intelligence very close to sentient humans, but not quite on the mark.

As far as I can recall, there was no speech, but I thought I heard things—mostly coaxing telepathic phrases, urging me to lie down with them.

I was saved by the legs of a huge golden bird striding into the grove, whose upper female figure equaled or rivaled the combined beauty of the Harpy, Kinnari and the tree's "Nariphs."

It was then that I realized how out of sorts I was. Whether it was due to the prolonged effects of a mortal breathing Himmapan air, or that I stood too near the edge of an entire Nariphon Orchard, I do not know. I was in the throes of a drug-like stupor and unfortunately, the next hour of my Himmapan birding is the stuff of dreams. The memories I write here are lamentably vague and regrettably confused.

I believe that I met *the* Kinnari Princess, "Manora (or "Manohara") of the story of Prince Sudhana in the *Divyavadana* (or my translation by N. J. Krom, *Barabudur: An Archaeological Description*).

I remember a conversation on the nature of enchantment, but little else. I think she was trying to jest that I had been compromised by the Nariphs. I returned an ill-conceived joke about whether or not she ever washed the "smell of humans" off of her (it was said in her tale that once she returned to the celestial kingdom of the Kin-naras, there were several baths to do just that). This could have been construed as rude—especially by a princess! Luckily, she laughed heartily and unlike the Kinnari of the gate, I remember Manora's laughter as charming and wholly human, which was great comfort while my brain was addled.

After such esteemed company, a parade of extraordinary denizens of Himmapan came to greet me. I may not remember all of what was said, but I can attempt to identify which ones I saw.

<hr>

Artist's / Transcriber's Note ~ 1: The Nariphon Tree is mentioned many different times throughout his journal. Interestingly, the outcome of being in its prolonged presence differs slightly throughout, as if he is unwilling or unable to recount the experience with any real precision, even to himself. There are definite hints that he "succumbed" and that perhaps this was one of the tributes that the Kinnari warned him of. The other possibility, which The Mythologist eventually adopts as his main theory (or excuse?), is that the tree releases powerful chemical agents, like pheromones, to "further its purpose on the hapless." The further details are collected in the volume themed on wondrous plants.

***Artist's / Transcriber's Note ~ 2: The Mythologist seemed to spend more than just a short amount of time in Himmapan. Further sections of his experiences include extensive encounters with Nāgas, Devatas and other creatures, all of which have been moved to be included in future themed volumes.*

Nok Hussadee

Bird Maidens of Himmapan

I was introduced to a cyclopean blend between bird, kinnari, and elephant. This giantess was the size of a barn, and I remember the clatter of over-sized golden jewelry as the grove quaked with her footsteps.

When featured in stories, a Nok Hussadee never misses a chance to demonstrate its physical strength, but she carried only a pool of water as her burden, cupped tightly in her hulking hands, which held the mobile environment for the amphibious Sintu Puksee, lest she dry too much in the sun.

Himmapan was like a relentless midsummer's day. It was hot and dry, and the air was full of stray feathers and glittering pollen. The smooth golden skin and metallic plumage of the maidens magnified the glare. It was a place of some magnitude, where everything had greater substance, save for me.

I do not recall confabulating with the Nok Hussadee. I remember her as mute, but full of gentle smiles and timid gestures. Despite her towering form, she seemed used to being around smaller, more delicate creatures. It's surprising how quickly I was able to relax.

Sintu Puksee

A water nymph was cupped in the massive hands of Nok Hussadee. Instead of shaking my hand, she performed back-flipping maneuvers and coiled her Naga's bottom half (a dragonish, eel's tail) into artful loops and flowing undulations. In my euphoric state, I believe I reached into her small pool of clear water to touch the ornamental fins which were her hair. They were cold, and like the quills of a porcupine...and dangerous!

She was a beautiful thing, but tipped in all manner of razor and spine. Her speech was attuned to aquatic converse, yet she tried nonetheless and pierced my ears with screeches and high-pitched chatter. She might have been the most excited of all of them to see me, yet for all of her animated exuberance, we failed to make ourselves understood in any way, shape or form.

Her Kinnari wings were the most intricate of all that I'd seen, and her coloring, despite being out of the water, was vivid. It was difficult to dilineate where her blue scales ended and her frayed blue feathers began. Truly a marvel to behold, and it stoked in me a great appetite for hunting the truth behind mermaid forms, despite my fear of deep water. It might have been the sighting of this water nymph that spurred me to push my luck here, to try and see more.

Sagoon Hayra

Bird Maidens of Himmapan

There was something dangerous about the bird-nagi. By strange morphology, her mid-section held most of the snakelike properties, and was forever in motion, as if the writhing serpent energy was hard to contain. She used this as a hypnotic swaying, matched to the strutting steps of her bird legs.

Once introduced, I could not take my eyes away. She mistook this as flirtatious, and later performed an artful and overtly seductive dance, while the others played woodwind instruments of unlikely shape and unearthly pitch.

My guess is that Nagi are as misunderstood in the tapestry of myth as snakes are in nature. After seeing her, I have no choice but to err on the side that paints Naga or Nagi forms as guardians of streams, heralds of rain, and symbols of fertility.

She was a force of nature, and I regret that I cannot recall what manners I used to make my exit from this scene. To spurn her without a proper and earnest explanation seems a frightening prospect to me now. I can only imagine that perhaps Manora stepped in.

I remember backing away from the heart of the grove, bowing low and thanking the maidens of Himmapan for receiving a mortal visitor so graciously. I could count myself lucky to leave not wholly changed by the experience.

I traced my steps over the same path I made into the Nariphon Orchard, but my tentative ability to concentrate was suddenly shattered by the roar of a feral cat.

Tripping on the root of an immense tree, I drew myself up, and came face to face with a bird bearing the heavy, striped head of a tiger. It was only the size of a German Shepherd, but it was instantly obvious that this creature could hunt, stalk and kill me with the same ease as a terrestrial lion. This was my wake-up call that not all mixed forms in Himmapan were of regal elegance, nor hybridized into intelligent, amorous women. It was said in the stories

Suea Peek

of origin that these creatures were the offspring of a magical moment when "hate was lifted" by the gods so that all living things might love and inter-meld in a celebration of life. While an interesting thought, it's in contradiction to all there is to know about nature. The varying sizes alone would make the prospect an impossibility. However they existed, it made sense in a vast forest ecology that some of them might end up more beast than being.

I believe it was a Suea Peek that gave chase, but now I know there are so many amazing creatures in the forest that there's no way to be sure. The ones documented in Thai culture and Asian legends are merely the tip of the iceberg.

I took flight in sheer terror of my predator, assuming I was allowed admission into Himmapan with the full intention that I never live to tell the tale of the one day that Indra let in the mortal wanderer. The feeling of running from a predatory bird was strangely familiar. I leapt from green hillock to mossy knoll, back toward the large banyan tree, hoping that adrenaline would counteract the ether of the grove. The Kinnari guardian was dubiously absent, but I swear I heard her tinkling laughter sprinkled in between cat roars and my gasping breath.

Was blood the final tribute? My machine hatch wears the four-clawed scar that would have torn my back asunder. It's another reminder to me now to always consider the dangers of my work. Nonetheless, I used the Omni to search out other nearby environments within the enchanted realm. I would stay in Himmapan as long as I could.

My last stop in Himmapan was toward a lonely cluster of torchlight, upon a snow-encrusted mountain peak. It could easily have been solely an earthly place, upon the Himalayan Mountains, but it would have been so isolated and difficult to reach by foot. Only the spiritually equipped might have suffered the climb to the ancient monastery, and believed what I saw inside.

The temple itself was somehow both modest and elaborate. Its boxy compartments were painted in red and white, the central of which was rimmed by gold leaf balustrades and hemmed with peeling sculptures of naga / kinnari forms. I saw the same creatures I recently kissed the hands of, in the flesh, now as only static sculptures.

I could not find a level place to land my craft, and so I didn't try, and lighted upon the smooth stone of their outer ledge instead. I banked on the good nature of the monks, and the

Shang—Shang

possibility that they would take my arrival as a boon or test of their Nyingma school. I might only be an emanation of the 9th vehicle, after all—a test toward understanding Dzogchen (Perfection).

Arctic wind swept up the mountainside and through me. Within minutes I was received both tentatively and excitedly by a flurry of red and orange robes. The younger monks led me to the austere seniors, who did not stand but remained in a meditative position, concentrating on their centerpiece, an artful statue of a shining woman with human, but feathered legs, and wings upon her waist. We were flanked by a chorus of throat singers and monks playing shawms and elaborate conch shell trumpets. The dirge was rhythmic and could have been the musical equivalent of the wavering stupor I had been in most of the day.

It took me a moment to realize that the statue was slowly coming to life. At first her movements were like sideshow animatronics, but soon enough, the being was able to move with grace, as if alive, and the pauses of their chanting were filled with the ringing of her hand cymbals (the "shang" bells).

A senior monk spoke to me, "Is this the first of many miracles that the man of the iron egg will bring upon us?"

This perplexed me, but I gave a respectful pause and replied, "I am forever grateful to witness the fruits of your devotion. She is your wondrous tulpa...not mine."

A tulpa is an animate manifestation of sheer will.

Eventually, their dancing thought-form stopped in her original pose, forever a golden statue again, and I left them to revel in the magic cast by their discipline.

With the warmth and splendor of Himmapin already long behind me, I set out for less enchanted hiking. Further on the theme of cold mountains, I would trade ancient Himalayan peaks for those in the Carpathian range, a bit further in the time line.

Wila

ALSO: Vila or Veela

I began my slow ascent into the Carpathian Mountains. The paths were lined by walls of snuggled larches, their needles making a thick carpet upon the desolate paths, which allowed me to pass quietly, and in reverence of the primeval forest.

The villagers continually warned me of "woods witches." I assured them that I am here only to do a little bird watching but they just shook their heads and clucked their tongues in disapproval. Their suspicions were doubled when I accidentally shelled out way too many coins for two freshly baked cakes, one of which I saved for the trail, just in case.

Of course I chose the mountain path that the locals were most afraid of. After miles of hiking through pristine meadows and over rocky hillocks, it struck me how silent my surroundings had become. I began to feel like the trespasser they had taken me for.

I was certain I had come to the right place at the right time, but the flitting spirits of nature would not manifest. I then did something desperate and stupid; I found the oldest, most gnarled birch tree on the side of the mountain, and carved my name into her ancient bark. Immediately, my dare was answered with a flash of lightning and thunder whose percussion knocked me down the mountainside. By the time I found the path again, I was drenched by the slush and sleet of an odd and sudden winter thunderstorm. For the first time, fears of freezing to death began to haunt

me. I turned back, toward the village, but my escape was painfully slowed by pelting torrents of ice. Clearly I had crossed a line.

I made it back to the scant open meadows I had hiked into only hours before, shovelling my boots through dunes of sleet. I kept an eye on the purple clouds that swirled above, mentally pleading for the storm to break, but it only worsened. My eyes were blinded by the frozen grit and falling needles of the tussled branches above, and I continually lost the path.

The taiga, which had so far been silent and empty of wildlife revealed strange and startling creatures who always seemed to lurk in my peripheral vision. A white wolf crossed the meadow in front of me, low to the ground, baring even whiter teeth. It was unimpeded by the snow and mud, and left no paw prints. In the next meadow, a snowy owl swooped overhead, its talons skimming my wool hat as if to snatch it away. I had been dulled by the panic and tumult of the storm. By the time a large, albino serpent swished across my feet, I caught on to what was happening in the woods. I was never meant to get out alive.

I fell to my knees, reaching deep into my backpack, hoping that the weapon I packed had stayed dry. I spent the morning perusing the village for such a weapon and chose it carefully, minding the quality and craft. I found it below my trail mix and bread. It was dry and somehow felt as though it was still warm from the hearth!

I crawled to the nearest larch tree I could find and flung my arsenal down upon its roots. It was a cinnamon babka, baked to perfection, and iced with rosewater and honey. I pulled my gloves off with my teeth, and forced my frozen fingers to tie silk ribbons around the cake. Then I sprinkled the edge of the plate with fresh blueberries from my trail rations, and larch needles from the ground.

By the time I had finished, I realized the air was suddenly thin and I felt the sun upon my cheek. I looked up and found no trace of the storm. I was dry and back upon the peak where I carved my initials into the old tree. A woman stood before me, tall and stone-still, as if receiving my stance as worship. She was a vision of beauty, naked and one with the winter sun and pale sky, so much that I had to shield my eyes from the light that shined through her.

She glanced down at my offering and her blue lips gave me the slightest smile. Was that the moment of forgiveness?

Then her glance fell upon the defaced birch and my foreign clothes. Her crystalline eyes seemed to crack and shatter, piercing me with the shards. I winced and bowed further at her feet, remembering the storm that was her wrath.

I opened my eyes to find that her toes were the talons of the owl I saw in the meadow, and the borders of her body were of many folding and beating wings. Her visage had become lost in all aspects of the mountain. I saw her for what she was—a raw and primal chimera of nature itself, whose love or fury is indivisible from every seed, claw or snowflake.

She let out a song that sounded like the sweet chorus of many birds. Their fluttering tugged at her shape and broke into flight. My ribbons and round cake were gone. The offering was consumed without eating, in a way I do not understand and for what purpose I'll never know.

Such is the way of the Vila. ' Warrior, enchantress, valkyrie, faerie and witch.— An elemental, whose mood may change with the wind...and I owe my life to a cinnamon cake.

My brush with the Wila had left me shaken. If I had disappeared in Medieval Romania, my body would have simply disintegrated in the bellies of wolves, most likely to her exaltation. Who would mourn my frozen bones? Who would know of the things I have done? And my vessel is set to go...*where*, if I expire mid-voyage?

I've grown tired of tracking incomprehensible beings, for the moment. I believe I have become mentally exhausted, beleaguered by so many bouts of adrenaline from so many close calls. I can not tell if I am well anymore.

It was time to go forward, instead of back ...something with less consequence, and perhaps an assistant to aid me for a time, for company?

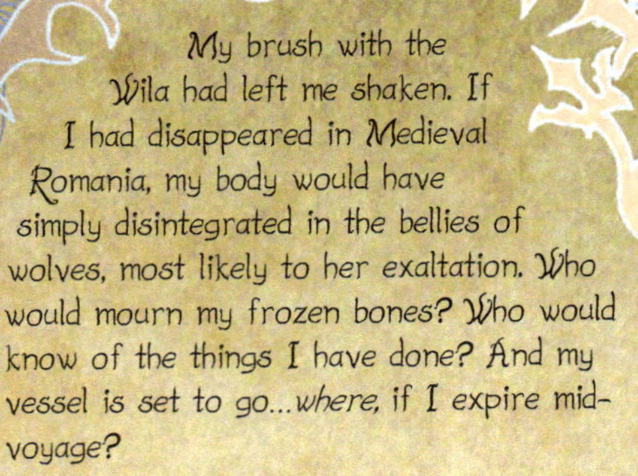

Alkonost

Adopting the 20th Century notion of "surfing" interconnected computer networks, I drifted through time, idly watching my search string for "Alkonost" fade to differing results through the many years:

8: The Greek demigoddess Alcyone had her body swapped for that of a kingfisher, for having playfully referred to her husband, Ceyx, as "Zeus." A time when pet names were punishable by omnipotent scorn!

860: Slavic mythology mentions the prophetic Alkonost as "a sister to the Sirin and the Gamayun," woven into their tale of creation.

1000: Medieval border illustrations—fantastic to behold! My favorite renditions, always.

1896: A notably beautiful painting, *Birds of Joy and Sorrow*, by Viktor Vasnetsov. He illuminated Russian folklore, which had assembled from eclectic sources and emerged unique, and in full bloom in the early 1900's. Perhaps I should see it fresh and shining at his easel? The boom was also accompanied by great poetry, theater, and music. The Alkonost is "capable of such sweet music, that you might forever forget all purpose and direction."

1910: Both the Russian and Medieval illustrations are recycled into Victorian postcards and ephemera, with syrupy romantic notions.

1952: A surprisingly well executed special effect of a raven-feathered Alkonost in the film "The Magic Voyage of Sinbad," by Aleksandr Ptushko (which was actually about the hero "Sadko" of the Russian epic tales).

1976: Scant appearances in table-top games, video games and cartoons, mostly as a monster (this trend continues on).

1995: A Russian heavy metal band who drew from folk music was named "Alkonost."

2018: An indie drama entitled "Alkonost" used the connection to the Greek myth tentatively to tell the story of a woman abused in her current relationship because she was happier in a past romance. The only connection is the theme of unwarranted punishment.

2032: The wealth of Alkonost art and cultural tidbits becomes clearer in the "Great Wikipedia Reboot" where all entries that ever existed were simultaneously revamped by pulling information from all search engines at once to be summarized by an unbiased artificial intelligence in one go.

2095: *Immersive Interactive Cinema* releases a 7-part, 100-hour "explorable series" on Greek mythology. It took five years to create, and was well received. Viewers are able to move through a 3-D experience within their living rooms, and choose what to explore. The original tale of the Alkonost is retold with aplomb.

Then, nothing significant until something caught my eye in 2313. A wealthy entrepreneur by the name of Ofer Rimokh was the first to showcase new technology that unified several emerging interactive technologies, all of which centered on machines "capable of reading brainwaves and applying creative algorithms *into* and *out of* the observer of 'something'" (the patent was hundreds of pages long).

It was touted as "a conversation *with* art." And most curiously for me, he chose the *1896* painting of the Alkonost and Sirin, *Birds of Joy and Sorrow,* to reflect the power of his new marvel. *This* is how I should view that painting. *This was my bread crumb.*

The painting was to be unveiled in Los Angeles, at the Consumer Electronics Show. For suitable company, I found a local university student, willing to overlook my clothing and demeanor, and be a part of crashing the unveiling. Easy.

Erica Masters was a "Future Studies Technology Development Engineer" and she flatly turned me down. *Not* that easy.

Cale Corbett, a pursuer of a Bachelor of Fine Arts degree, overheard my request, and was more than agreeable. I daresay he was inebriated by several substances as of early afternoon and found the parts about "possible breaking and entering in the name of art" the most alluring. I agreed because he was a painter and this was, after all, going to be a "conversation with art."

Days before the great unveiling, Cale and I found fairly easy access to the painting, by the roof of a building adjacent to the convention center that was about to host the Consumer Electronics Show. This building was to be the pre-show storage facility. It came down to some sophisticated lock-breaking, which nearly tripped alarms. Ultimately, we found our way into the proper storage area by hovering at the window, and cutting glass with an instrument of Cale's that I didn't recognize.

The advanced painting was set to operate the moment its coverlet was pulled away, but the only signal that it powered-on was a slight white strip of LED light at the top of the gilded frame, which in the pitch-black storage room was quite bright. There was no noise, and for a time, Cale and I just looked at the painting and back at each other. It was, by all appearances, a nice reproduction of the *1896* painting, sized to almost sixty inches wide. The frame was made to look antiquated, but I could tell by looking behind it that it was a thin-skinned reproduction that hid whatever wireless machinations were needed within.

Ensuring I would know how to operate it was why I brought Cale along, but now we were both stuck. He rolled his eyes at me when I asked about a manual, and I at him, when he waved his hands in front of the image for the twentieth time, using the same hand gestures that purportedly commanded his home electronics.

Finally, we located a tray of fifty or so, individually wrapped "Cranial Read Sleeves" or "CARS," as their sealed cellophane packaging stated. It seemed, without one of these translucent caps one cannot be a part of this blessed conversation with art.

I was beginning to doubt the magic. That was, until I stretched the rubber hat over my hair. The effect was instantaneous and unbelievably jarring. In the millisecond it might take to flick on a light switch, I was suddenly standing on a sandy beach, in blinding sunshine. I could feel the heat and the spray of the ocean as it lapped my shoes—or I should say, *a remarkable ocean*—since it was more or less styled after ink and watercolor, animated with all the frothing of low tide. I could smell salt air, and my feet felt wet!

'Truly amazing, and once again, I am defaulted to a principle that should haunt me time immemorial, the third of Arthur C. Clarke's laws:

"Any sufficiently advanced technology is indistinguishable from magic."

This was magic with voltage! My mind was not so much "invited" to enter this world, but was *harnessed* to do so. It did not take concentration, or a suspension of disbelief. They had finally created a portable dream world, and, no doubt, it was enslaving those parts of the brain that manufactured dreams to make the place seem real. Except that, perhaps most extraordinary of all, it was shared as well. I waded over to Cale, who was musing over some fanciful seaweed that was placed equidistantly throughout the tide. He was tugging at it, and found that it would stretch the way that we assumed seaweed does, but that it would never give entirely. This seemed to confound him, and he fixated on it, to my dismay.

"Let's wade to the Alkonost before we try breaking the illusion, *please?*" I pleaded.

"'Way more believable than my games at the dorm—*way beyond!*" Cale said. "Man...I don't have to tell you—I am tweaked out on this. This is not just a conversation with art. *This is the future.*"

"You'd be surprised how often that's said," I replied. "But, I do know this is some *part* of the future. I honestly haven't looked into it until now."

(I do *not* believe that Cale believed I was a traveler out of time, but my Omni vessel had convinced him I was at least interesting enough to follow into this.)

We walked toward the Alkonost, and in the distance, her melodious song became audible. This place was nothing like walking into *Birds of Joy and Sorrow* though I suspect this was by intentional design. Perhaps a simple beach was easier to display than a forest? Perhaps they wanted to show off the visceral nature of a painted ocean? Ahead, however, was indeed *an* Alkonost of "Joy." She was easily twice the size of us, and amazingly detailed. If there was a unit of resolution (pixel, voxel or polygon?) then surely their budget was spent mostly on *her.* Every filament of every feather was there, as she sang into the blue sky above. I could even see the humidity condensing into droplets on her iridescent plumage, as if her feathers were water-resistant. I remember thinking, "They've thought of everything," but I suppose, at some point, part of the credit for orchestration goes to the raw computation of the life-mimicking math.

She was perched upon a golden metallic knot that matched the gilded frame around the physical painting of origin. As the song went on, the frame slowly rose and encircled her, and twisted back through the ocean, forming into towering, abstract fractal driftwood.

Her song was some sort of orchestral arrangement, mixed and spun according to the musical fashion of the time. It had a chorus that spoke of love and longing. It was trying to be high-concept and many other things all at once, which was ironic, hiding inside the skin of a simple and eloquent painting from 1896.

Suddenly, a huge red logo came slicing through the ocean, parting the sea before us to declare their company credit: "7th Axis, Inc."

I told Cale that I thought this meant that the presentation was over. This was probably the point at which they stop and switch out for the next twenty or so onlookers at the convention. There were only so many of the Cranial Sleeves at the ready.

Somehow, I felt less compelled to continue to be there, inside their dream space. I believe I could have taken off the sleeve at any time, if I had tried hard enough, but I was compelled *not to do so*, until the end of her song.

But Cale wasn't ready to let up. At first, I was glad, as I admit I wanted a closer look at *her*. They (the creators, artists, and programmers) must have anticipated a few stragglers would try doing this, and creepily, the Alkonost looked down at us as we stared at her. There was something implacable in her gaze. I felt the weight of many centuries of technology culminating. I could feel the grinding of her proverbial cogs and gears by the inexorable march of progress...and the irony that they stuffed this into mythological taxidermy was too much to comprehend.

In her expression was the smirking gaze of insentient, artificial life. I needed to understand her but she would be unburdened by the question. We stared at her unlikely blue body, shuffling on her tangled, golden perch. She invoked all the emotions and narrative ponderance of contemplating fine art. At her great stature, her full bared breasts loomed heavily and heaved as she breathed. Her face was crafted with laugh lines and age. There was the aspect of "mother," or perhaps "mother nature," in her gaze, which makes even less sense to me now, unless she is the mother of all things on the brink of false life...and of false nature.

Cale, on the other hand, was unwilling or unable to be moved, due to the jading effects of everyday encounters with similar computational farce. Where I saw art and felt reverence for her as an accomplishment, he saw only the next iteration of what was nostalgically still referred to as "video gaming." He climbed her perch, which caused her heavy, crowned head to jerk downward at him, with the speed of an inquisitive bird. I remember thinking this was going to be some sort of test or "first contact" between homo sapien and "Frankenstein's Bird." Was Cale the first villager to come into contact with the roaming monster, or was he Igor, the assistant of the doctor, who one could imagine, would have stolen any moment he could get to molest the corpses when the doctor's back was turned?

Regrettably...it was *the latter*.

Without pause he groped one massive blue breast in his palm, and then squeezed and slapped at it, musing at the sway of its volume. He laughed gleefully, remarking down at me, "Oh man...*You gotta feel this*. It's like...*100%* real. *Unbelievable*...They finally got it right. Touching these should be their whole demo!"

The Alkonost looked down at him with a curious expression. At first I thought he managed to break the illusion, but she narrowed her eyes. Was that the look of precalculated, scripted offense or was an illusory, monstrous bird interpreting perverse, unwanted advances and inventing an affronted response? How much had the creators of this pocket world prepared for?

Alas, I will never know. Extreme events followed...

Did you

Siren

The sun began to set in fast-forward, as if in the mad motion of a time-lapse recording, and the sky went the color of scarlet fury. The clouds were like tissue paper, sopping blood...

The Alkonost evaporated, and her golden framework began to twist into monstrous forms, and scissor itself apart. An immense shadow fell over the deepening sea.

I felt the tug of mental gravity again, as if I was compelled by a foreign will to stay where I was. My chance to depart had been granted, and then revoked. It was like being in the nightmare of another person and at their mercy as to when they might wake and release me. I suddenly hated the idea of the enslaving cranial sleeve. I was wearing a brain-shackle, donned by my folly with eager amusement.

I had little time to admonish Cale, and instead opted for a warning, "This might be some kind of security breach awareness. I can't will myself out, now, can you?"

Cale was clearly terrified, which surprised me. Perhaps his constantly unimpressed demeanor was a front for a more fragile mind? In the face of real danger, I had come to regret the age of my partner in crime. I used him to ensure my ticket to this illicit puppet show, with no exit strategy nor regard for what might happen if we were caught, or became part of the act.

YOU'RE GOING D

The tall shadow breached the horizon. One stilt-like leg marched deliberately over the other, and splashed hard into the frothing surf. She wailed some kind of screeching, mind-melting, operatic distortion. It wavered between melody and an electro synth train wreck. She was the sister of the Alkonost, but not the gentle Sirin—this was the dark *Siren*, known time and again as a storied villainous temptress. She was the luller and lurer of hapless sailors to death upon jagged atolls, to be impaled by the wood of their own splintering ships. A Siren casts a long shadow indeed!

Her lower half was that of water fowl, with stork legs like 20-foot, Roman columns. She was upon us, and aware of our presence beneath her, and gazing down, she bulged her eyes and sang louder still. I could feel the spit from her crescendoing notes, and their pitch was like white lightning in my mind. Pain was a possibility in the simulation, after all...unlike in sweet, untinged, REM nightmares, for which I then pined. Had that been lightning in my mind, or in the dream, or in the short-circuit of the program? Or, *all of the above?* The question added to the numbing headache.

There was a roiling thunderstorm in her wake, and a typhoon over the sea that quickly became a water spout. We were drenched and then drowning.

I thought of Odysseus, who was obsessed with hearing the siren's song. He bid his sailors plug their ears with beeswax, as they tied him to the mast. He begged to be untied, so that he might throw himself into the sea for the singing sirens, but they only tied him tighter.

I found the elastic mock seaweed, and stretched two branchlets into my ears, pushing as hard as I could. I yelled at Cale to do the same, so loudly I thought my throat might split.

In myth, the end of the Siren's song meant death. Like Odysseus, I eluded her song, and so shattered her spell.

The scene cleared to white static, and I tore away the cranial sleeve. Cale was not so lucky, as I found him catatonic and drooling, what I'm terrified to admit, seemed like sea water.

Amidst the technological possibilities, the event had either been the hidden side-project of the ambitious creators, an anomalous malfunction, or...as I suspect, some sort of elaborate security protocol, with a terrifying dramatic flair to ensure that an unlawful voyeur would remain entranced long enough to be discovered and arrested.

I made it out just before the arrival of authorities. As far as I could tell, Cale was...eventually rehabilitated, and absolved of crimes due to the piteous state of his traumatized mind. The debut of the device was cancelled until many years later.

Despite the grim outcome, the fact that I had escaped the same way as Odysseus exhilarated me. I must eventually investigate what's to become of this technology.

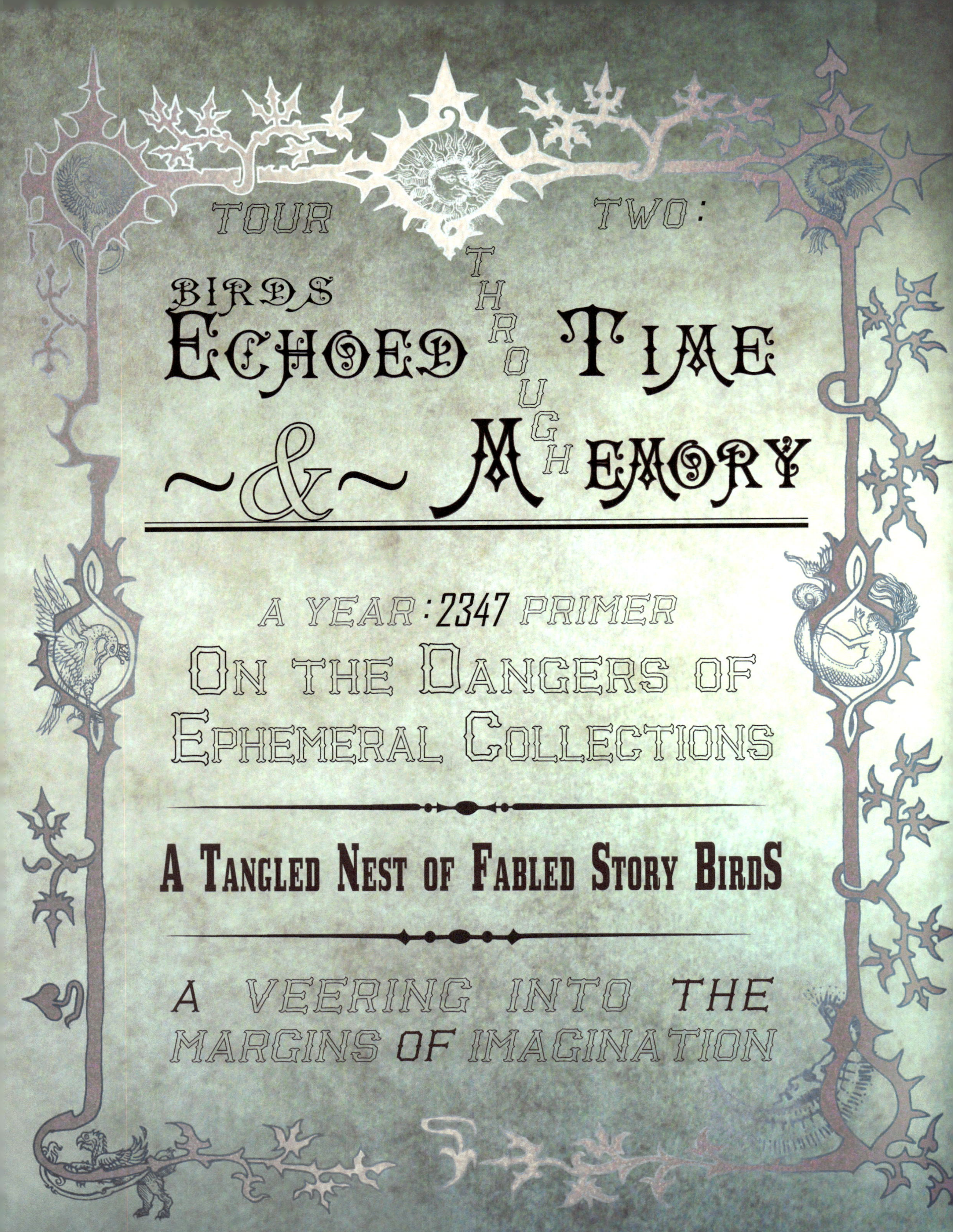

TOUR TWO:

BIRDS ECHOED THROUGH TIME ~&~ MEMORY

A YEAR: 2347 PRIMER
ON THE DANGERS OF
EPHEMERAL COLLECTIONS

A TANGLED NEST OF FABLED STORY BIRDS

A VEERING INTO THE
MARGINS OF IMAGINATION

SPLENDID

My journeys seemed to culminate in the darkest ends. Are all tales merely candy wrappers for poisonous trifles, as in those musing cautions spun by Jacob and Wilhelm Grimm?

I cannot allow myself to become superstitious. No knocking on wood, nor avoiding years ending in 04...or 13. For if I go down that road, my line of work is so poised for false wards, evil eyes of protection, and unlucky pitfalls that I would be quite paralyzed to do anything at all.

I decided to look into the supernatural side-stories of a few common, everyday birds.

Egyptians believed that pelicans knew the safest paths to the underworld for the freshly dead. They branded them lucky and able to turn away snakes (they do eat snakes opportunistically).

Indian folklore told of a mother pelican who murdered her nestlings out of frustration. She was so regretful after, that she impaled her own breast with the tip of her beak, and resurrected her chicks in a shower of blood.

The medieval Christians were so sure of this magical self-sacrifice, that they filled their bestiarial entries with praise for the pious pelican, be she ever so Christlike:

Pelicans

Like what tender tales tell of the Pelican
Bathe me, Jesus Lord, in what Thy Bosom ran
Blood that but one drop of has the pow'r to win
All the world forgiveness of its world of sin.

—St. Thomas Aquinas

The only way to be certain is to see for myself. Choosing my time carefully, I clamored along a bank of barnacled stones, once again huffing chilled, viscous ocean air. This time, it was not a facsimile, so my eyes burned and my nose ran.

I tried something that felt more verboten than most of my current misdeeds, approaching a semi-famous historical figure, a painter (a skilled royal miniaturist, actually) by the name of Nicholas Hilliard. Nicholas was known for adding to the pelican dogma by iconizing Queen Elizabeth I as a mother willing to sacrifice for her people. He painted a pelican broach in the center of her elaborate dress, for which the painting is nicknamed.

He was alone, studying a pod of pelicans only fifty or so feet away. After careful introductions (and flattery for his work), I asked him what he had learned from watching them. He told me excitedly that more than once, he saw with his own eyes that "the mother pelican wounds her chest to feed her offspring—as in page one of the Holy Scriptures." (He must have been speaking of the illustration of the pelican in the King James version.)

I stood there, quietly, for some time, trying hard to view the world through his lens—a distorted glass that still included alchemy and elixirs—but all I saw was a pelican feeding its young from the stretching membrane in the bottom of her beak.

And so we parted, two men of differing eyesight. And for once I am unchanged, unrattled and uninjured, though having collected no magic from the world.

I took to sifting through mythology for fragmentary notes about cormorants. Their mention is scant. Overall, it seemed the world's bards couldn't decide if they were a talisman of good, or a dark omen. Perhaps that should be my query?

On the side of "wrong," in John Milton's *Paradise Lost,* Satan gained access to Eden in the form of a cormorant, branding the bird a trickster before ravens and crows usurped their spot ever after. But Satan's disguise is not the fault of cormorants, surely? In Ireland, a single cormorant upon the steeple of a church is a foretelling of bad luck, but luck is a fickle thing in the Emerald Isle. With so many omens per day, it would be hard to keep track of one's score of fortune.

Yet there is much and more on the brighter side of their coin. In China, cormorants were used as trained fishing birds well into the 21st Century. Their necks are tapered with bands to prevent them from swallowing what they catch. Even the fishermen who did not use them painted their boats in cormorants.

Cormorants

In all things faerie, one *might* assume chaotic neutrality, or even goodness, before malice. In the epic tale of Ulysses, our hero incurs the wrath of Neptune, who aims to break him with the worst storms imaginable. The sea nymph, Ino Leucothea, delivered a belt made of woven, deep-sea plants that would grant him invulnerability. She chose to rise from the depths in the shape of a celestial cormorant. Most alluring is the Norwegian fairy tale of the Island of Udrost, said to appear to the fey or those with second sight. It is the latter that I chose to investigate.

I slid back 1400 years from where I had been drifting in warm sunshine, to the freezing waters surrounding Lofoten, a scattered archipelago so far north it brushes the rim of the Arctic Circle. I skimmed the waves with my Omni Traveler with little regard to the handful of wide-eyed sailors. I believe my craft to be water-impervious and able to dive, but I decided against toying with those features. Also…I am not fond of deep water. Perhaps my imprudent approach to ancient times should be thought of as reckless, but I believed it to be *irresistible* to the insatiable curiosity of the Fey Folk and their ilk, and I have been right so far.

For the day's effort, there was nothing. 'Little else than chunks of steaming ice, deep blue water, and lonely solitude. My thoughts turned to gloomier things, which matched the spreading twilight. As I was about to give up, my bright beams touched the ruffled, glistening feathers of a gulp of cormorants—much to my delight. If I could not walk upon grassy, green Udrost, then I would end my day with an observation of these birds in the wild. Yet there was something wholly eerie about them. They sat idly sharing one piece of knotted driftwood, staring back at me and giving no sign that they might attend to the business of the sea, and what should be their stopless task of catching anchovies.

In the company of suspected fairy-kind one must often try the humiliating task of speaking to animals. I stated boldly, "It is said that a trio of cormorants brings word from the dead. *Might this be your purpose?…Or, are you emissaries of grand Udrost?"*

They stared just long enough for me to question my own sanity. Then, in the green glow of my head lamps, I saw their gawky throats quiver in the effort of speech. Each bird took a few croaking words, in succession, until the sentences formed:

"Your necromancer—bids you—hello…Mythologist. He was not—as keen—to see those birds—as you. May the rungs—of your ladder—have teeth that bite—he sayeth—loudly and often—where he is, nowww."

And they flew from their flotsam into the last gasp of twilight and disappeared entirely.

Hercinia

"Follow the grandfather oaks" was the only tip scribbled among the margins of all my copies of the olde texts. Modern historians agree that one ccn approximate the Hercynian Woods by crossing the Rhine River in Germany and traipsing into the fringe of the Black Forest. As usual, I needed to find the core fragments of what was left of yet another place that blurs the lines between life and legend.

Carelessly waltzing into vast wilderness without aid or guide is foolish. Purposely starting the hike at dusk is vastly idiotic. It wasn't long until I realized the magnitude of my arrogance.

Amongst the tallest oaks, the trail disintegrated under a millennia of fallen leaves and the chaotic patter of elk and reindeer. I was instantly lost, with a waning lantern and no moon. In mere hours I was reduced to choosing my direction at random and began following the tiny lights of fireflies from tree to tree. At least it was a warm and summery night to which I would walk to my doom.

Perhaps it was this true abandon that led me upon a copse of trees, hosting small arboreal beings, whose wondrous feathered bodies lit up their canopies in a ceiling of eerie, yellow light. I immediately assumed that the quills of their feathers were churning in the same enzymatic biolu-minescence of the fireflies. After a while in their presence, I was allowed to hear their "music," which was like the unmoored, looping chaos of mockingbirds. Yet it was this noisesome piping of their reed instruments that lit them in the gloom, and guided me to safety.

It was time to see what became of the "mind exploration technology" that I had experienced in 2313. I think I was stalling the inevitable draw of such a veritable playground. The idea that I could stop sifting texts and simply waltz into a virtual environment to interact with intelligent mythology intrigued me. Even if it was an obvious abbreviation of life, or some sort of animated search engine result, I had to see more of this. I wanted to fill the most impossible gaps in my improbable birding endeavor.

I thought I should jettison ahead and spend days dialing through the history of the future. I should do my homework, and read about the outcome, pinpointing the best year and the best day…and I started to do just that:

2321: The first true "Dream Rooms" draw crowds for miles from around the

THE BLUEBIRD OF HAPPINESS

globe by promising an unparalleled experience (similar to what I saw with the Alkonost).

2344: Interconnected Home Dream Rooms begin to allow users to experience, and/or add to, the cumulative Mass Virtual Library, or the MVL in their media rooms at home. The hardware required for Dream Rooms was shaped like a sprawling circulatory system, with a thick central wire that resembled a vein, and subsequent branching wires mapping the room's space. It was because of this, and the tendency of personal virtual collections to resemble chaotic holographic scrapbooks, that the MVL was nicknamed "The Ephemeral Artery" or the "Eph," for short.

2379: The first attempt at integrating true, *not virtual*, mentally-programmable matter with the Ephemeral Artery begins in choice test rooms.

2383: The entire endeavor in this form seems to cease…(?)

The further a list like this goes the faster things change, technologically. It's a bit like opening a potentially great book and reading the last five pages first. I have a vague, nagging recollection that "reading ahead" doesn't truly work for time transgressors, as usually the traveler alters the time line the moment they embark. And, at any rate, what would be the point of being unstuck in time and space if I were only to read about life after the fact?

I decided I should try to bring more capable assistance this time. I thought that someone for whom technology like The Ephemeral Artery might be commonplace and even passe could be of use. I embarked on the risky business of skirting the 5th millennium. Thus far, years in the early 4000's are the farthest

WIDE-AWAKE
EL CARPIO
HGH
MALL
RED SIN

I've ever dared to go. There are...complications with time breach awareness soon after the turn of the 41st century, and there is already a contract out for my seizure.

In 3999, amidst an air of great excitement and the typical rallied electric hope for some sort of great societal change, I met Ivy Lane. Young, at twenty-eight, and even younger at heart, I saw a great enthusiasm for my offer to tour time in search of improbable things—especially since, in her year, the Omni Pods were coming to fruition. Ms. Lane was something of a living fossil, herself. Though she possessed a sharp wit and a good mind, she had been the final pursuant of her era for a degree in folklore and mythology—something her peers deemed as useful as a glass hammer. This alone was reason enough for me to meet with her. I profess to enjoy her company immensely, even though she set the high price of exhausting every possible incarnation of unicorns, before she agreed to tour an early Ephemeral Artery. In her time, the Eph had indeed become a thing of forgotten trends, replaced by virtual reality feedback implants, and similar thrills provided by nanotechnology stuffed into oral capsules, set to safely expire after so long. Programmable matter was never again tied to something so arbitrary as the human imagination.

Next, I made the mistake of becoming acquainted with Doctor Antonius Braxton II, the world's preeminent expert on the history of The Ephemeral Artery. Ivy and I attended his lecture, and were impressed by his thorough comprehension, yet, even he had gaps and mysteries needing resolution. It took an extensive song and dance to convince him that I possessed a craft worthy of time travel. By the time we left for our primary tour, Braxton was still quite agitated by my proposed reason for using my craft and my out-of-place clothing.

We started in 2334, during the heyday of The Eph as a world phenomena, but the lines were too long. Waiting becomes irksome when one might skip through time. Being deprived of his chance to be there at the beginning, it was from then on that Dr. Braxton became outright sullen, pompous, and short of temper.

Instead, we skipped ahead to see first-hand, the result of later Ephemeral Testing Stations and why they were abandoned in their glory. We found a later Ephemeral chamber in the US that had been suddenly decommissioned one year before our arrival. We worked out an elaborate plan of breaching the facility that ended up being totally unnecessary. Did this mean that people were afraid to try to loot them? Or that no one knew it was hidden there? Or, perhaps it was that secret Ephemeral stations were so entirely unremarkable on the outside (they were just large, white buildings, rather like warehouses) that no one knew where they really were.

Our exercise in breaking and entering was clumsy—especially on Braxton's part. I took one tentative step into the vast, abandoned space and suddenly realized that I was indeed nervous to interface with the Ephemeral Artery. Each time we had passed it by along the time line, I think I had been a tiny bit relieved.

My footsteps echoed and clacked upon what looked like dusty, black linoleum. It was like an immense empty warehouse on the inside. I could see that the structure was cut into and under the surrounding hills, as if to conceal such a cavernous internal space. I also noticed that the room was no longer a sterile environment, as hundreds of spiders had taken residence high above us, their cobwebs drifting downward, like the ghosts of Spanish moss. I wondered what else might have moved in. Might we be gnawed by rats while we stumble about in the dark, unable to see them due to a virtual immersion that robbed us of the most basic true-life awareness?

There was a pedestal by the door on which rested a black metallic sphere. Dr. Braxton waved his hand over it, and red pin lights awakened within. "All those exploring must now place their hands over the sphere until the light turns green," he said, with calm insistence. I could tell he was eager to begin.

"That's it?" I asked. "Are you sure? There is no other mechanism?"

"That is all," the doctor said, with finality. "The Eph was an elegant creation by this time. No implants or temporary nanoparticulates needed."

Ivy offered to stay out of our first jaunt to watch the door and make sure everything went OK. We emptied our pockets into a small satchel whose sole contents before that was three bottles of water. She set the little bag by the door and sat down to watch.

I tried hard to remember anything that might allow me to comprehend what I was about to see, but the only thing I could think of was my one waking dream-gone-nightmare, with the Alkonost and the Siren...my "bird of joy," and my "bird of sorrow."

Indeed, as before, REM sleep was a more suitable parallel than all of Braxton's description. I turned to Ivy, and asked her why no one mentioned dreaming as a way of explanation, but she only cocked her head and furrowed her brow, citing that most people had long since given up most dream-sleep in exchange for more working hours and free time by way of advanced pharmaceuticals, and, *"hadn't I?"*

That unsettled me for many reasons, but I hadn't much time to dwell upon what she'd said until now. I hold dream-time as sacred. I had been rudderless without the dream of the Gamayun. I daresay my mind is not keen without beloved illogical inspiration—what is our reason without its colorful counterpart? What is science without creative inspiration? Certainly, I stood on the brink of the marriage between infinite mathematical calculation and what I'd hoped would be the apex of human expression in art—The Eph. Ivy Lane's generation was one so inwardly-consumed that they'd traded most natural creative nourishment for a few more hours of quantum computer entertainment. Perhaps that's why so many of their technologies seemed more like vanity mirrors, with increasingly sharp focus. Was the Ephemeral Artery also only a mirror? Was I about to be startled at my own mental reflections and comically so, like a puppy barking at itself in glass? I thought, not for the first time, of the Victorian psychomantium side shows, and felt foolish. Psycho-mantiums used rooms coated with mirrors and low, strobing light to induce a trance-like state, or what is known as the Ganzfield Effect.

Psychomantiums had their roots in ancient Greece. Oracles concocted theatrics for their labyrinthine temples. The people inside these oubliettes were invited to stare into a pool of blood, said to be a portal to another world, until they would hallucinate "something" (later called "catoptromancy"). The Grecians were quite impressed and paid their catoptromancers handsomely. Surely, three millennia would offer better tricks?

There was nothing for a time, then a hum all about us. I remember seeing the black orb hover overhead, spin like a globe, halt and spin again, in seemingly random opposing directions. Tiny red lights multiplied within, like angry bees building a hive in fast-forward. There was a sensation of fainting, but not falling. Suddenly, I was standing in a green meadow. For one disorienting moment, there was no sound at all and I feared the mechanism had destroyed most of my senses while interfacing. Dr. Braxton flickered into being beside me, muttering a command in code that was unintelligible to me. He forced the sound to unmute and explained that whoever used it last must have turned it off entirely.

The meadow was no longer unsettling. It was breezy, natural, and enclaved by identical rolling hills, which seemed to carry on for miles around us. It was overcast, as if it had just rained. I could even smell the dew nestled between the sweet, high grass and felt a longing to sit down and comb my fingers through it.

"Go ahead," Dr. Braxton said. "We're here." He took a dramatic deep breath, "This is the high-point of the Eph. Explore the genius."

"Does this device...*fuse* our minds as well?" I asked, not relishing the notion of my mind being the Siamese twin to Braxton's head.

"It's more like a heightened awareness. Hive-minding has only just begun to be possible in *my* time. Don't worry. Worrying just makes the dreamscape all the twitchier. We've got to relax, and let the Eph taste our minds to get things rolling."

I pulled the grass. It was cold, and moist. I splintered it between my fingers and examined the green pulp. "This is all inside my mind?"

"Mostly," said the doctor with a magnanimous grin. "That, and programmable matter. But your mind helps fill in the gaps. This hilly terrain we are standing on—it's literally sculpting the room, faux atom by faux atom, but only building the surfaces it needs. To Ivy, on the outside, we probably look like we are standing about twenty feet above her, walk-ing over shifting, black plastic blocks that are ever-refining their resolution around us. It's quite magnificent to behold from the outside-looking-in, as well."

I had turned away from my green-stained fingers to listen, and when I looked back, the pulped grass had vanished, as well as all sensation of moisture, but not before I felt a pin-prick. Later, I would find a tiny black splinter lodged in my skin.

Braxton urged me to try my first visual search string and make a "mind field." He told me to focus inside and then speak clearly toward the horizon. I thought for a while, then spoke simply, "Birds...of lore."

The hilly terrain vibrated and flattened, and then began to fold and unfold into an ever-increasing number of three foot by three foot luminous squares, laid into a neat grid before us, *stitched into the very earth!* It was an overwhelm-ing orchestra of motion. If that wasn't enough, each square tile then began to revolve various imagery at three-second intervals, as if more and more results were jostling for my attention, so that I may refine my query. This reaction was what the machine was created for, and it seemed eager to play. Speaking my search was like firing a pistol at a starting line, and now the race had begun.

It was, admittedly, exhilarating. The human mind finally triumphing over matter. I felt like a wizard able to move a mountain with the flick of my wrist. I was in the state of awe that Dr. Braxton so smugly assumed.

More and more images from throughout time flooded my mind field. By "guessing" my will—perhaps by monitoring my brain waves, the Ephemeral Artery began culling out more modern references and so I simultaneously muttered my refined challenge to it. It was to be a bird so obscure...so abstract and impossible to see "in the flesh" that I was sure its conjuration would clog the gears of the machine and leave us stumbling in the dark, empty warehouse. I yelled at the grey horizon, grinning stupidly, *"The Bluebird of Happiness!"*

Once again, the reaction was instantaneous. The grid began flipping its tiles like falling dominoes. Images of Victorian ephemera began to flood the field first. Digitized replicas of paper cut-outs of birds, cherub-laden valentines with cheerful blue birds in the margins, scrolls of poetry featuring bluebirds, illustrated lyrics to a 1934 song by Sandor Marmati, a person-sized puppet of a feathery yellow bird shown painted blue and singing a song, lyrics shown over a music video by a band labelled "They Might Be Giants" from 1990, more lyrics, more nostalgia, but no single Bluebird of Happiness could be culled out—not even from 5000 years of accumulated art.

To the far left there sprouted a branch of tiles focused around the science of bluebirds. Their migration patterns were diagrammed. Also their diet, mating habits, and several tiles devoted to the fact that birds with blue feathers are *not exactly blue at all*—their feathers evolved hollow space that acts like a prism chamber, reflecting only blue waves of light from the sky to our eyes. One tile showed their extinction in 2213, and their gradual resurrection from cloning in 2309.

To the far right, the origin of the bluebird as a positive symbol is being debated between tiles. The Navajo identified mountain bluebirds as an incarnation of the rising sun, but there were a few "antonym" type tiles shown, with many "blue birds of unhappiness," perhaps just in case. These featured opposing instances of blue birds depicted in less common ways. Many were heralds—like guiding symbols, which led to another tile—a grim story by H.P. Lovecraft in which an azure bird was the lure to an abyss and the prompt toward destruction. I made a mental note of that tile...and lingered on the others. Even the songs.

It was all too much...but none of it was what I had hoped for, after all.

I turned to Dr. Braxton, who had long-since been exploring his own smaller search strings, "surfing the Eph" as he called it, and I said, simply, "I was under the impression that the atoms would...assemble my legendary creature, more or less on command. Is that not what happens here...or?"

Dr. Braxton rolled his eyes, "You are expecting a lot considering your query. Here, *watch me.*"

He held out his hands, as if to cup something fragile, and said, "*A* Bluebird of Happiness."

As if from nowhere, a vivid bluebird appeared nestled in his palms. The scene was similar to the masterful Disney animated films featuring a princess who cannot stroll a meadow without bluebirds alighting on her shoulder. Of course, that made Braxton into Snow White inside my mind, which made me laugh. It started chirping its natural bird song, which, half-way through, began to morph into the 1930's orchestra song, and then the Navajo chant, and even the song from the 1990 band, the only parts of which I could make out were: "Bluebird of friendliness...it's always near...Blue Canary in the outlet by the light switch...Who watches over you..."

Braxton gave me the look of a kindergarten teacher, showing a child how to color inside the lines. "Beautiful. See? You said, '*THE* Bluebird of Happiness...Instead of '*A* Bluebird of Happiness.' It's ok. It's a rookie mistake. You'll get it."

Within his dreamt-of playground, the doctor had taken on his most obnoxious tone yet. I don't think he truly wished to share his precious moment in time with this pure incarnation of the Ephemeral Artery. I, on the other hand, was beginning to want out altogether.

I started my backpedal, politely, "Well...I see the potential here, but...if I cannot conjure these entities as a spirit amalgam, or a tulpa, then I have no use for this place. It's scarcely more to me than a psychomanteum."

The doctor ignored me from then on. After a time, in defiance, I yelled "*The one…the only…Bluebird of Happiness!*" at the horizon line, and without waiting to see the result, turned to say, "Shall we go, then?"

Dr. Braxton was red-faced. He had been nurturing a zealot's devotion for the Ephemeral Artery, and while standing inside this model, which he had deemed the apogee of their line, there would be nothing but reverence for this particular oracle.

He rolled his eyes for the umpteenth time that day, and sighed, "I've only known you for a short time, but do you even realize how ridiculous you are? *Scribbling* on *paper?* Driving what must be stolen technology *randomly* through time…for what? Some kind of snipe hunt? How can you stand in the face of mankind's greatest artistic invention, at the point where it was at its most undiluted—"

The unseen machinery let out a groan and then a rumble, followed by what could only be described as an earthquake. The knolls we had been standing on gave way to more of the flat, smooth grid, knocking us down. This allowed my query results to expand in all directions. There was something odd about the perceived voids of space beneath the flipping grids—a flickering that was unkind to the eyes. The particles that made our surroundings showed through, pulsing and taking on a burning blue phosphorescence, as if ice could be stoked like the embers of a blue bonfire.

The sound went awry as well, skipping and jumbling into a cacophony of tangled, bluebird-related audio. I could hear parts of that song again…" *I'm your only friend…I'm not your only friend…But I'm a little glowing friend…But really, I'm not actually your friend…*"

Through this storm I could hear the doctor yell, "Awwwww…It's a 'blue-screen!'" They were supposed to have been weeded out decades ago. Really Eph? *C'mon?!*"

"What do we do?" I asked him, concerned. The Ephemeral Artery was real and present. It was the ground, the air and the sky above. Watching it begin to disintegrate was not much different than being caught in any other earthly disaster event, but the uncommon sort—like being next to a melting volcano. My heart was in my throat.

"Run for the door…if we can."

But we'd been walking through our visual search fields in all directions for hours. We had become immediately lost in the Eph, suctioned-in, like so many others before us.

I yelled out for Ivy—our fail-safe, lookout, and chief backup plan, but when I called for her, I heard her near me, instead of across the room.

Ivy answered, tremulously, "Right here. Sorry, guys…It turns out that it takes considerable effort for anyone on the floor, to stay out of this Eph. I was sucked in ten minutes after you started. I've been here, quietly surfing my own mind fields. It's a lot different than the watered-down version I know."

Now I was disgusted, and a little more than unnerved. "Are we stuck here, inside the Ephemeral Artery?"

Braxton indignantly barked, "Now, hold yourself together. I'm sure this sort of thing was accounted for. And you have *me* here to fix things, not that I would ever call her *broken*. We are more broken than *she*, my friends."

He brought up the hidden user interface again, and began arranging strings and typing commands on a floating keyboard. Meanwhile, the Eph seemed to be doing its own jig. Like a broken record, it was looping that part of the song again and again, "*I'm your only friend…a little glowing friend…I'm not actually your friend*"

"Something's coming," Ivy said, and for the first time I realized she was truly afraid. I had never seen fear cross her face in all of our practice trips—not once.

The horizon, where we had been speaking our queries, was ablaze in a blue aurora. Then, from a far off distance, I could see the shape of a massive bluebird. It was strange—like an amalgamation of many parts of the various bluebirds from my searches. Most of it was right out of Victorian paper craft but it was holding a flag in its beak, as if from the examples portraying blue birds as heralds.

"It's a herald of doom," I said, half-joking. But when the absurd creation was upon us, it was the size of a small airplane, and it was a solid thing, matter-made, not an interpolated phantasm. We were all knocked asunder and fell downward, somehow plunging between the gaps of the grid, where there should have been no space to fall through.

Forever
Stay

WIDE-AWAKE

We dropped at least forty feet and I was certain this would be our true demise—thrown into the gaping maw of a hungry sentient dreamscape! *A fitting end for me.*

I should have known that the cat would not let its captive mice die so easily. Not so strangely, our fall was broken by the verge of

Cu

a forest path. As we tumbled through thick, snapping brush, my thoughts turned to regret for putting Ivy and Dr. Braxton in harm's way. I hoped none of the snapping I heard was a compound fracture, yet my fears were confirmed when the doctor yelled out that he must have broken his arm. A great bit of clumsy first-aid followed, with next to nothing to help him but a makeshift sling, made from parts of my jacket, and a stick to keep his arm stiff. Ivy left the small bag "elsewhere."

Bird

Had it been left "upstairs?" In another chamber?

Or, had we not truly fallen through a floor at all, and the damned thing was sitting next to me, cruelly obscured, beside the exit door, *the whole time?* That was a distinct possibility in the Eph. It may have slowly built up the floor of the chamber, beneath us, micron-by-micron, only to drop us to the bottom of the very same room we began in.

I tried peppering the bellowing Doctor with reasonable questions:

"How was it possible that we'd taken this plunge? Had he ever heard of experimental Ephs that had multiple chambers, towers or dungeons? I asked."

When he finally calmed down, he answered, "Never. Because a lower chambers means that what just happened, *would happen*, all the time, and the number of injury lawsuits would go through the roof. *Blast it all!* Maybe that's what shut them down. Overreaching bastards! Oh *damnit*—my arm...my arm, *is throbbing.* I've never been in this much pain in my life!...Thank you, Mr. Weird Cosplay, and Madam Misadventure, for such a wonderful day. *This is all your fault.* All. Your. Fault."

I paced the odd, mossy glen, trying to scope the depth of the hazy forest, and trying to squint my way through the dim, blue twilight to see what was next.

Ivy seemed to be in shock. Under her breath, she muttered, "That blue bird. It was some kind of monster. You can't make weapons or monsters that are free to act under their own constructed

behavior sets in my time. There are locks, and fail-safes. That thing, was, for all intents...real enough to kill us."

I said, "Maybe." The Doctor began an annoying diatribe on how her rudimentary grasp was misleading her, between dramatic gasps of pain.

I remembered what Braxton said about light hive-minding, and how it might use our thoughts to perpetuate the illusion. "Doctor, can't we simply walk together, in one direction until we feel the true wall of the space we are in, and then inch across until we find a door?"

The doctor, sputtered indignantly, "Pfft—please! That's the first problem they solved. She'll just make a curved coating over the true wall that gently leads you in another direction. Remember, in my lecture, the part about 'Elegant Oblietteing?' *Everything* here is designed to keep you in suspended belief. I will run exit commands on her and get us out of here. Try not to think of any of your crazy, made-up garbage, or this twitchy, broken Eph will just make it for you, *again...*and then *who knows?!*"

I didn't say anything, but that part terrified me. Even when I am relaxed, most nights, I would give a gold clock to be able to stop my mind from working over-time. So, I tried my darnedest to think of all things benign—trees, clouds, grass. Alas, my string of thoughts quickly turned to something like this instead: "Pillows. Down. Feathers. Plumage...Birds." And then, fearing which bird creature might pop into reality next, I tried to switch to something different, but all I could think of was my former comparison to mirrors and how the Eph seemed like a glorified psychomantium. The harder I tried to blank my mind, the worse it got, and before I knew it, the forest was alive with the strange calls of unseen birds.

Ivy and Braxton immediately shot me daggers with their eyes. I could only shrug apologetically, mumbling, "What can I say?...I have had birds on the brain, of late."

Ivy approached me slowly, as if I were a toddler clutching a weapon of mass-destruction. In even tones, she said, "For now, why don't you just tell us one of the *nice* bird myths that you had hoped to see in here. Caaarrefulllly."

I did feel like I was carrying a loaded weapon. My mind reeled—my internal list of legends and lore spinning like a wheel of fortune. Before I was aware that I had chosen something, we were already in the presence of a small, exotic bird...speaking Spanish between chirps, of course, as birds do.

I decided to approach it. I would try to take the brunt of any dangerous conjuration and fall on the grenade. In the center of our glen, the little bird sat, staring intently at its own reflection, its small head pivoting to and fro, in the inquisitive mode of bird-curiosity. I was once again reminded of catoptromancy and the Grecian oracles of olde.

But this was the Cu Bird—the star of a little Mexican Folk Tale about vanity.

"I think we're good, for now," I said, making a show of my exhalation, as if I had succeeded in safely concentrating. I understood that everything that happened from here on out, could erupt into random and violent living nightmares, fed by the ferocity of our stressed imaginations, and that's all there was to it.

I continued, "The story is, this little bird was naturally plain in plumage and coloring, so it took on the task of "bird messenger" for all the forest. In turn, the council of birds paid the Cu Bird one feather each, which the Cu wore with great pride, and vanity, as he was so enthralled as to scarcely leave his reflection, and he shirked his duties as messenger. The council meetings were riddled with missing or confused birds who never got their summons. The eagle of the council grew angry, and started a great, cacophonous argument with all the birds he could find."

I paused and put my hand to my ear, expecting to hear such a simulated cacophony, but the forest was mostly silent. I got the odd feeling that the Eph was also listening to my story.

So I went on, " Their noisome squawking woke the God of Forests, so he sent a bird emissary to quiet them down. That emissary was ignored in the fracas. Ignoring gods in folk tales results in nothing nice, and so, the God of All Forests—Quetzacoatl...or B'alam, maybe? He took speech away from all birds, period. The rest of the birds blamed Cu Bird for their newfound silence and therefore promised severe retaliation. And the ironic moral is, now the Cu Bird may only show itself at night when no one or no thing can see it."

As I finished the tale, I stroked the smooth, soft little feathery head of the Eph's approximation of a Cu Bird. This made Ivy smile and put us at ease a bit. I was not going to let the Ephemeral Artery become a frightful poltergeist if I could help it. The Cu Bird flew off suddenly, giving us a start. Braxton collapsed the floating, translucent user-interface windows he had hacked open, having failed to gain any ground.

"What a load of crap," he sniped, clutching his broken arm. "Legends and kiddie bedtime stories might have broken the Eph, and gotten us into this, but science and clear thinking will get us out."

I responded, "And so? Do we have a plan? Tell me, how does a session with crazed Ephemeral Arteries usually...end?"

The Doctor's brow furrowed in that way that showed he was about to admit there was a flaw in his fondest of creations. "Well...the watered-down, neutered models in my time just *know* when you want to end the simulation or you can say 'end.' Don't bother, though. I already tried that a while back. You can force-quit from the floating UI, which I can successfully bring up, but it doesn't respond half of the time. I remember reading that test station Ephs sometimes could only be shut down from an external observation / control team. Once, there was a known incident where a test subject was accidentally left in long enough to die of dehydration but that shouldn't have to happen here, in *this* model. I'll show you why."

The Doctor limped over to the pool of water that the Cu Bird had been lovingly staring into.

"I thought it was your *arm* that hurt?" I said, grinning, but he was less than amused.

He stared at the pool, and commanded, "*Pure water only.*" He reached down and cupped some to drink. "The basic elements of nature had to be the first chemistries of programmable matter." He took another swallow, but seemed distracted by something in his reflection—his Latin complexion turning ruddy, and then pallid. Suddenly, he choked hard and spit out a bloody shard of the black calcified resin, just as I had found lodged in my finger from the faux dewy grass.

"Are you alright?!" Ivy said in alarm, but Braxton had been more shaken by what he saw in the pool than the malfunction with the water. He ignored her, and began walking down the path.

I called to him, "Doctor, what did you see in the pool? Tell us what you saw!" But he would not talk about it again.

We walked the ominous path, laid out by the Ephemeral Artery for some time—long enough that we should have long-since outpaced the dimensions of its housing, tenfold. It was getting darker in the forest, and I found myself at the mercy of Doctor Braxton's knowledge, yet again. I asked him if this seemed normal.

He didn't answer me at first. Eventually, he spoke into the air using the most basic, original syntax for commanding the Eph. He even pro-nounced each forward slash" as he went.

"Synthesize: 3-dimensional / functioning_prop / electronic_device / flashlight." Nothing happened. He opened a floating UI window, and again, as if from out of nowhere, a slice of the air seemed to peel away. He repeated the command upon a glowing, projected keyboard and a silver LED flashlight, circa 21st century, finally appeared in his hand. He almost fumbled it, but caught it, and turned it on, shaking it at me. His smug look of triumph was short-lived, however, as, in an instant, instead of a flashlight, he was holding the leg of a stout barn owl. Startled, he jumped backwards, and the large owl flew into the tree tops in a huff. "That's great, he grumbled. "That's just great...

Aosaginohi

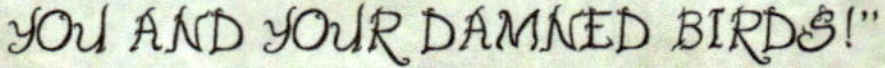

YOU AND YOUR DAMNED BIRDS!"

No one said a word for a long while. Then, Braxton answered my original question.

"All Ephs keep an Earth-time cycle of night and day, but it's not always in line with the outside, real time. Depending on the software iteration, some were advanced enough to keep the time and simulated cycles of other known planets or other time periods on Earth by request of the user. Say, for instance, the Silurian Period, around 400 million years ago, which had much shorter days. I can't remember what time it was outside when we entered, but I think this one's off-kilter."

"Much like the rest of it," Ivy said, in consternation. Her criticism went ignored. Braxton was becoming increasingly introspective, which worried me as much as anything else.

"Well," I began, "We can't be stumbling through the woods in the dark. Ivy, let's see what you can think of to light the way?" I issued it as a challenge, with a lop sided grin. We walked on for some time, but she was continually quiet. "I guess mythology students of the class of 3995 leave much and more to be desired. I weep for the future, as it were."

"Shut it!" she said, laughing. I do have one, and it's on your theme of birds, too. I tried talking to the Eph in my mind but nothing happened."

Braxton cut in, under his breath, "Don't be too sure."

As we came over what had (coincidentally?) been the highest hill in a long while, we saw the land change in a valley below us. The whole forest was squirming, shuffling from oak and spruce, into tangible approximations of artful Asian flora as if they had grown straight out of Japanese woodblock prints. What had been an empty gorge was now a picturesque stream with rivulets of water diffusing the creek bed like the bleeding strokes of a Sumi Brush.

Was Ivy's vision this keen, or was this the Ephemeral Artery flexing its muscles?
"Breath taking," I declared. "If only I could see more of it in the dark. Ivy, what is this?"

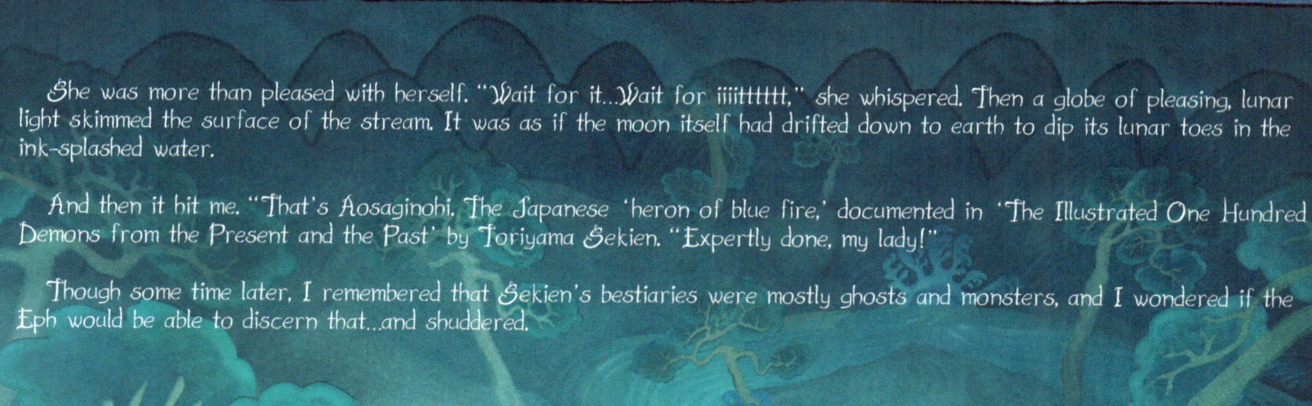

She was more than pleased with herself. "Wait for it...Wait for iiiittttt," she whispered. Then a globe of pleasing, lunar light skimmed the surface of the stream. It was as if the moon itself had drifted down to earth to dip its lunar toes in the ink-splashed water.

And then it hit me. "That's Aosaginohi. The Japanese 'heron of blue fire,' documented in 'The Illustrated One Hundred Demons from the Present and the Past' by Toriyama Sekien. "Expertly done, my lady!"

Though some time later, I remembered that Sekien's bestiaries were mostly ghosts and monsters, and I wondered if the Eph would be able to discern that...and shuddered.

Sirin Wedding

"We followed the luminous heron as it fished the stream throughout the artificial night. No one mentioned sleeping, as the prospect meant trusting the space we would sleep in (which we did not). At best, it would be rest with one eye open and it seemed better to keep going, trying to think of a way out, or hoping that simply by moving forward, the simulation would run itself out. The Doctor had agreed that might work.

Braxton had become so quiet that I asked him things just to check in. He had only one epiphany throughout the rest of the night that caught my attention.

He wondered aloud, "What if this wasn't a normal Ephemeral Artery after all? We wandered in, like flies to a spider, and it could have been one of the lesser known alterations, like...to run a custom experiment?...Or worse, a military variant."

"A weaponized Eph? C'mon," I said," doubtfully. "To what purpose?"

"Nobody knows," he replied, clutching his arm and wincing again. "There were rumors, but the military, of course, never owned up to any of it. The idea might have been to run tests on the limits of human sanity. Some said Ephs were used abusively in interrogations, like locking a prisoner inside a nightmare until they snapped. Others said, fantastically, that Ephs were used to desensitize soldiers to bizarre or improbable combat encounters, in the event that the enemy might unleash spliced genetic monsters. There were even stories that the military thought the Ephs might hone their psychic soldier projects. I don't mention the negative applications in my first lecture. Maybe you two should have taken my whole course before we went, half-cocked, back through time to break into a random experimental Eph that's clearly out of its gourd?" Braxton broke into the maniacal laughter of a man at the end of his rope.

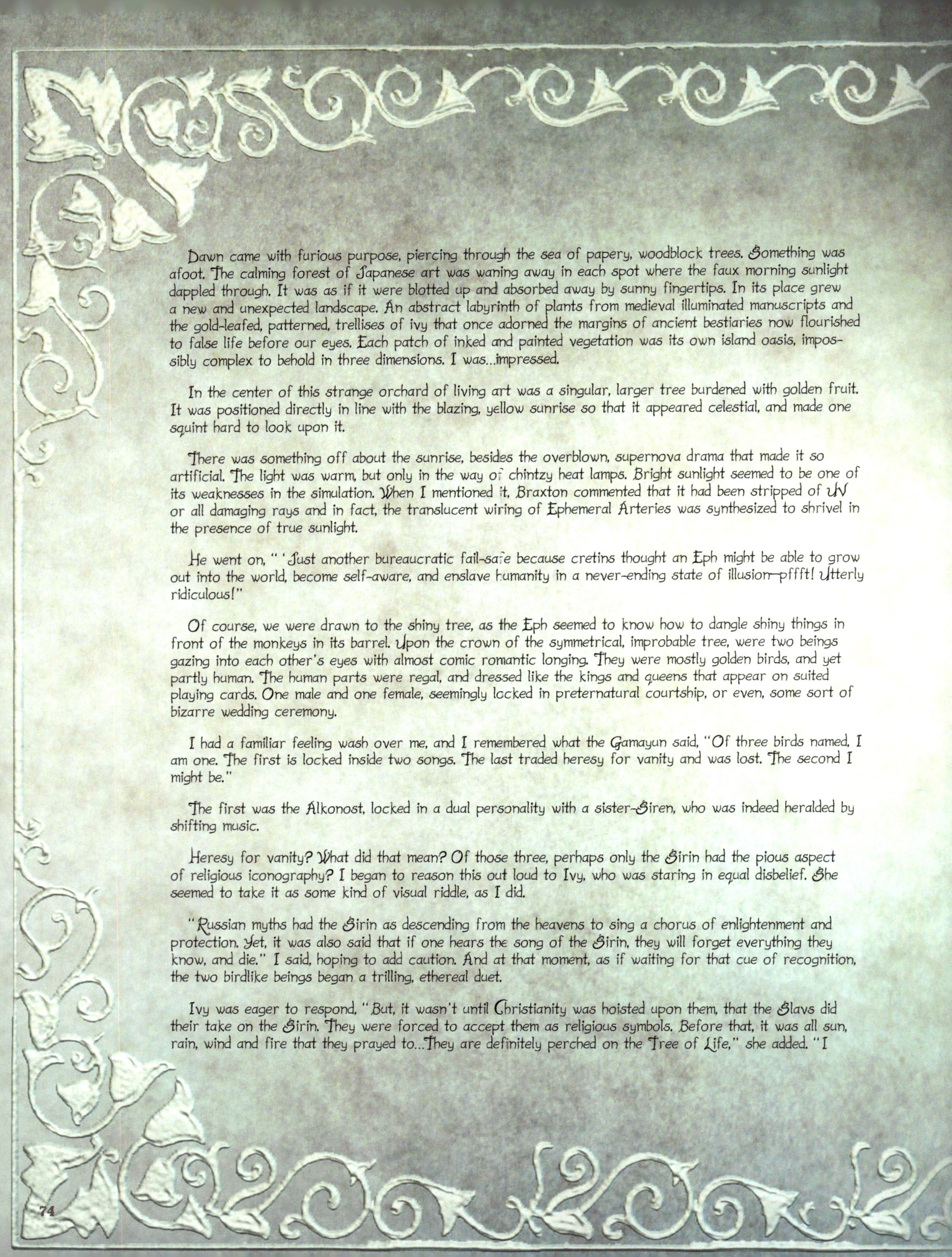

Dawn came with furious purpose, piercing through the sea of papery, woodblock trees. Something was afoot. The calming forest of Japanese art was waning away in each spot where the faux morning sunlight dappled through. It was as if it were blotted up and absorbed away by sunny fingertips. In its place grew a new and unexpected landscape. An abstract labyrinth of plants from medieval illuminated manuscripts and the gold-leafed, patterned, trellises of ivy that once adorned the margins of ancient bestiaries now flourished to false life before our eyes. Each patch of inked and painted vegetation was its own island oasis, impossibly complex to behold in three dimensions. I was...impressed.

In the center of this strange orchard of living art was a singular, larger tree burdened with golden fruit. It was positioned directly in line with the blazing, yellow sunrise so that it appeared celestial, and made one squint hard to look upon it.

There was something off about the sunrise, besides the overblown, supernova drama that made it so artificial. The light was warm, but only in the way of chintzy heat lamps. Bright sunlight seemed to be one of its weaknesses in the simulation. When I mentioned it, Braxton commented that it had been stripped of UV or all damaging rays and in fact, the translucent wiring of Ephemeral Arteries was synthesized to shrivel in the presence of true sunlight.

He went on, "'Just another bureaucratic fail-safe because cretins thought an Eph might be able to grow out into the world, become self-aware, and enslave humanity in a never-ending state of illusion—pffft! Utterly ridiculous!"

Of course, we were drawn to the shiny tree, as the Eph seemed to know how to dangle shiny things in front of the monkeys in its barrel. Upon the crown of the symmetrical, improbable tree, were two beings gazing into each other's eyes with almost comic romantic longing. They were mostly golden birds, and yet partly human. The human parts were regal, and dressed like the kings and queens that appear on suited playing cards. One male and one female, seemingly locked in preternatural courtship, or even, some sort of bizarre wedding ceremony.

I had a familiar feeling wash over me, and I remembered what the Gamayun said, "Of three birds named, I am one. The first is locked inside two songs. The last traded heresy for vanity and was lost. The second I might be."

The first was the Alkonost, locked in a dual personality with a sister-Siren, who was indeed heralded by shifting music.

Heresy for vanity? What did that mean? Of those three, perhaps only the Sirin had the pious aspect of religious iconography? I began to reason this out loud to Ivy, who was staring in equal disbelief. She seemed to take it as some kind of visual riddle, as I did.

"Russian myths had the Sirin as descending from the heavens to sing a chorus of enlightenment and protection. Yet, it was also said that if one hears the song of the Sirin, they will forget everything they know, and die." I said, hoping to add caution. And at that moment, as if waiting for that cue of recognition, the two birdlike beings began a trilling, ethereal duet.

Ivy was eager to respond, "But, it wasn't until Christianity was hoisted upon them, that the Slavs did their take on the Sirin. They were forced to accept them as religious symbols. Before that, it was all sun, rain, wind and fire that they prayed to...They are definitely perched on the Tree of Life," she added. "I

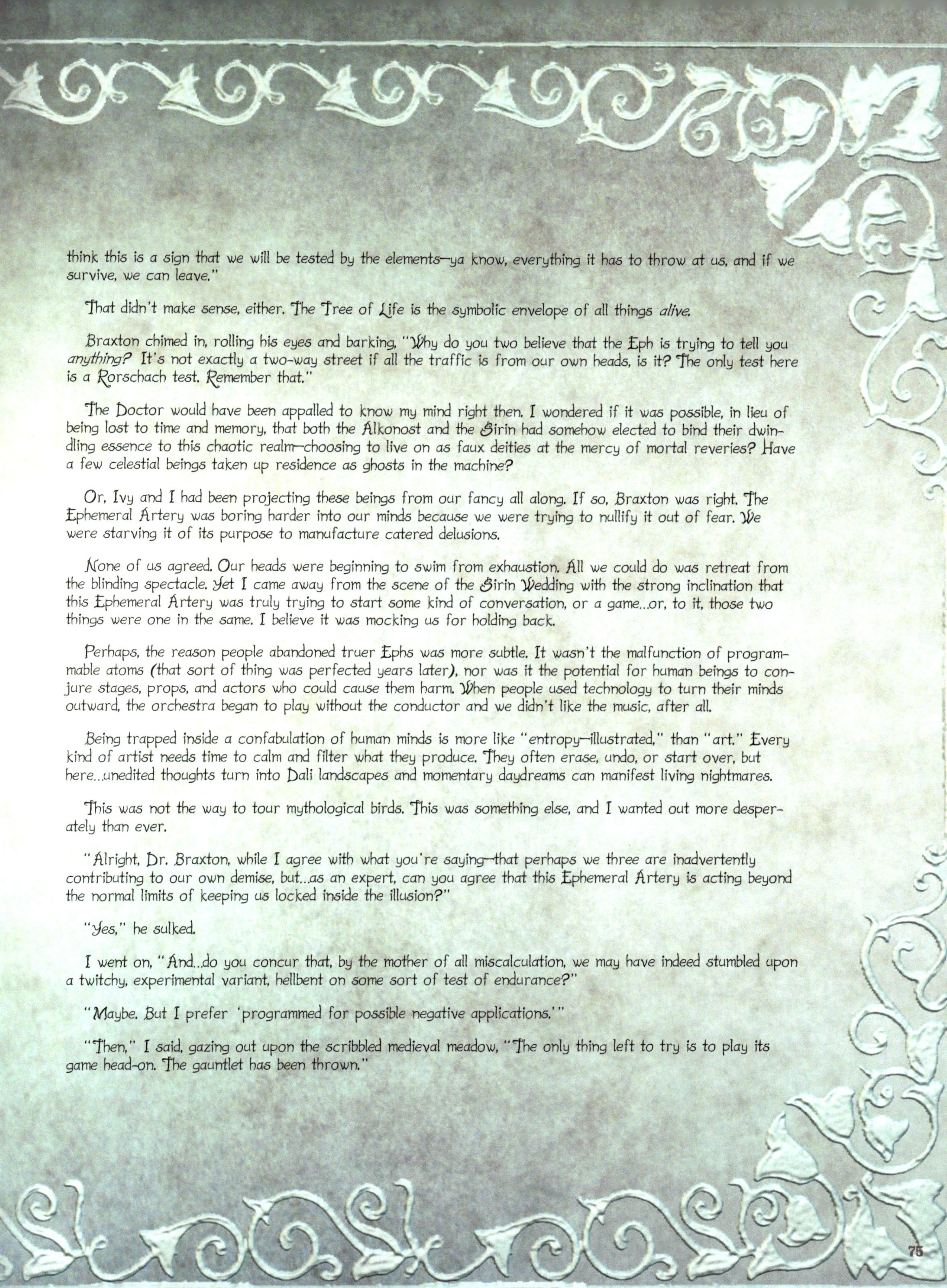

think this is a sign that we will be tested by the elements—ya know, everything it has to throw at us, and if we survive, we can leave."

That didn't make sense, either. The Tree of Life is the symbolic envelope of all things *alive*.

Braxton chimed in, rolling his eyes and barking, "Why do you two believe that the Eph is trying to tell you *anything*? It's not exactly a two-way street if all the traffic is from our own heads, is it? The only test here is a Rorschach test. Remember that."

The Doctor would have been appalled to know my mind right then. I wondered if it was possible, in lieu of being lost to time and memory, that both the Alkonost and the Sirin had somehow elected to bind their dwindling essence to this chaotic realm—choosing to live on as faux deities at the mercy of mortal reveries? Have a few celestial beings taken up residence as ghosts in the machine?

Or, Ivy and I had been projecting these beings from our fancy all along. If so, Braxton was right. The Ephemeral Artery was boring harder into our minds because we were trying to nullify it out of fear. We were starving it of its purpose to manufacture catered delusions.

None of us agreed. Our heads were beginning to swim from exhaustion. All we could do was retreat from the blinding spectacle. Yet I came away from the scene of the Sirin Wedding with the strong inclination that this Ephemeral Artery was truly trying to start some kind of conversation, or a game...or, to it, those two things were one in the same. I believe it was mocking us for holding back.

Perhaps, the reason people abandoned truer Ephs was more subtle. It wasn't the malfunction of programmable atoms (that sort of thing was perfected years later), nor was it the potential for human beings to conjure stages, props, and actors who could cause them harm. When people used technology to turn their minds outward, the orchestra began to play without the conductor and we didn't like the music, after all.

Being trapped inside a confabulation of human minds is more like "entropy—illustrated," than "art." Every kind of artist needs time to calm and filter what they produce. They often erase, undo, or start over, but here...unedited thoughts turn into Dali landscapes and momentary daydreams can manifest living nightmares.

This was not the way to tour mythological birds. This was something else, and I wanted out more desperately than ever.

"Alright, Dr. Braxton, while I agree with what you're saying—that perhaps we three are inadvertently contributing to our own demise, but...as an expert, can you agree that this Ephemeral Artery is acting beyond the normal limits of keeping us locked inside the illusion?"

"Yes," he sulked.

I went on, "And...do you concur that, by the mother of all miscalculation, we may have indeed stumbled upon a twitchy, experimental variant, hellbent on some sort of test of endurance?"

"Maybe. But I prefer 'programmed for possible negative applications.'"

"Then," I said, gazing out upon the scribbled medieval meadow, "The only thing left to try is to play its game head-on. The gauntlet has been thrown."

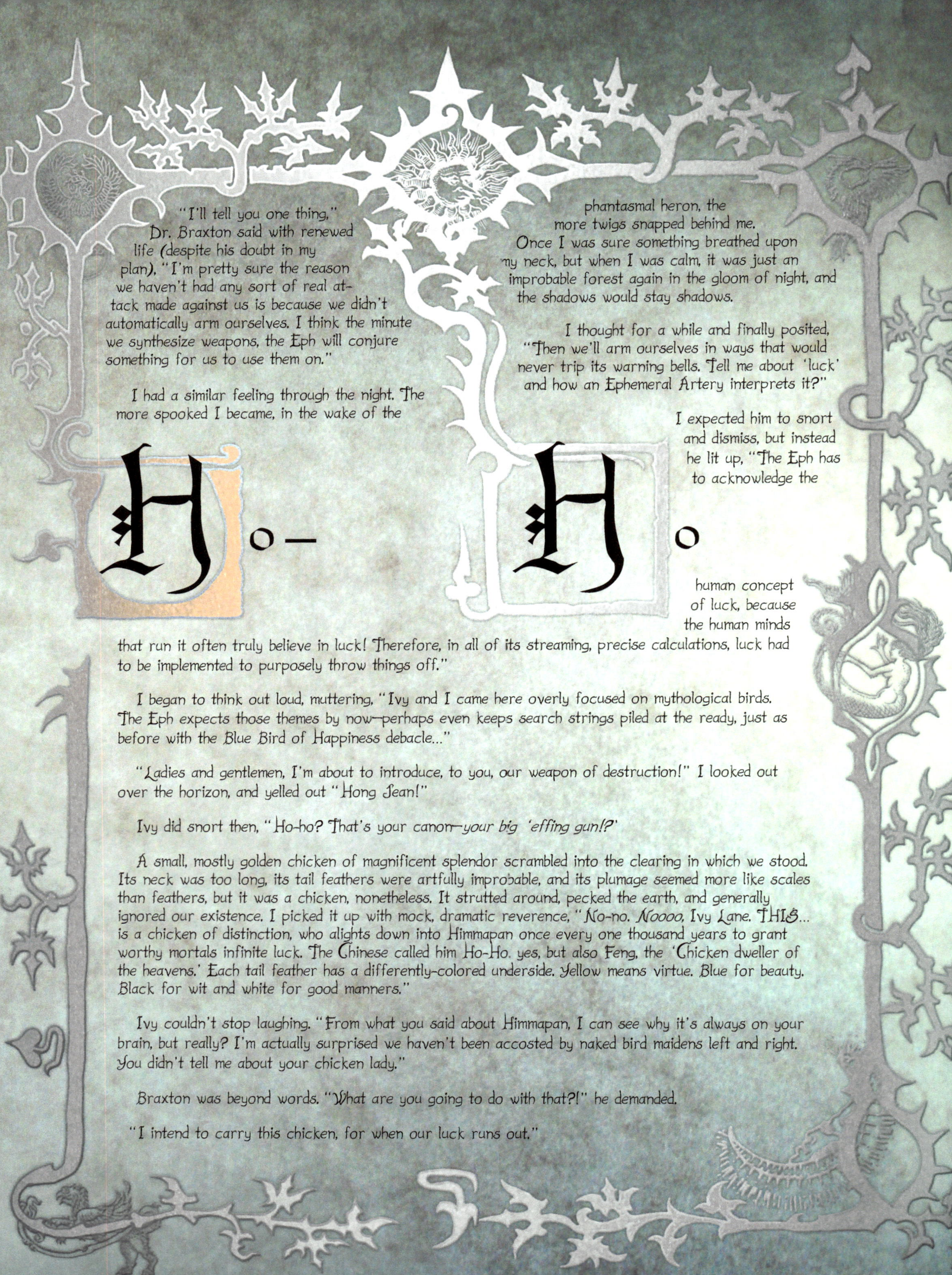

"I'll tell you one thing," Dr. Braxton said with renewed life (despite his doubt in my plan), "I'm pretty sure the reason we haven't had any sort of real attack made against us is because we didn't automatically arm ourselves. I think the minute we synthesize weapons, the Eph will conjure something for us to use them on."

I had a similar feeling through the night. The more spooked I became, in the wake of the phantasmal heron, the more twigs snapped behind me. Once I was sure something breathed upon my neck, but when I was calm, it was just an improbable forest again in the gloom of night, and the shadows would stay shadows.

I thought for a while and finally posited, "Then we'll arm ourselves in ways that would never trip its warning bells. Tell me about 'luck' and how an Ephemeral Artery interprets it?"

I expected him to snort and dismiss, but instead he lit up, "The Eph has to acknowledge the

H₀- H₀

human concept of luck, because the human minds that run it often truly believe in luck! Therefore, in all of its streaming, precise calculations, luck had to be implemented to purposely throw things off."

I began to think out loud, muttering, "Ivy and I came here overly focused on mythological birds. The Eph expects those themes by now—perhaps even keeps search strings piled at the ready, just as before with the Blue Bird of Happiness debacle…"

"Ladies and gentlemen, I'm about to introduce, to you, our weapon of destruction!" I looked out over the horizon, and yelled out "Hong Jean!"

Ivy did snort then, "Ho-ho? That's your canon—your big 'effing gun!?"

A small, mostly golden chicken of magnificent splendor scrambled into the clearing in which we stood. Its neck was too long, its tail feathers were artfully improbable, and its plumage seemed more like scales than feathers, but it was a chicken, nonetheless. It strutted around, pecked the earth, and generally ignored our existence. I picked it up with mock, dramatic reverence, "No-no. *Noooo*, Ivy Lane. THIS… is a chicken of distinction, who alights down into Himmapan once every one thousand years to grant worthy mortals infinite luck. The Chinese called him Ho-Ho. yes, but also Feng, the 'Chicken dweller of the heavens.' Each tail feather has a differently-colored underside. Yellow means virtue. Blue for beauty. Black for wit and white for good manners."

Ivy couldn't stop laughing. "From what you said about Himmapan, I can see why it's always on your brain, but really? I'm actually surprised we haven't been accosted by naked bird maidens left and right. You didn't tell me about your chicken lady."

Braxton was beyond words. "What are you going to do with that?!" he demanded.

"I intend to carry this chicken, for when our luck runs out."

CHICKEN
CELESTIAL
OF LUCK!
HO
HO

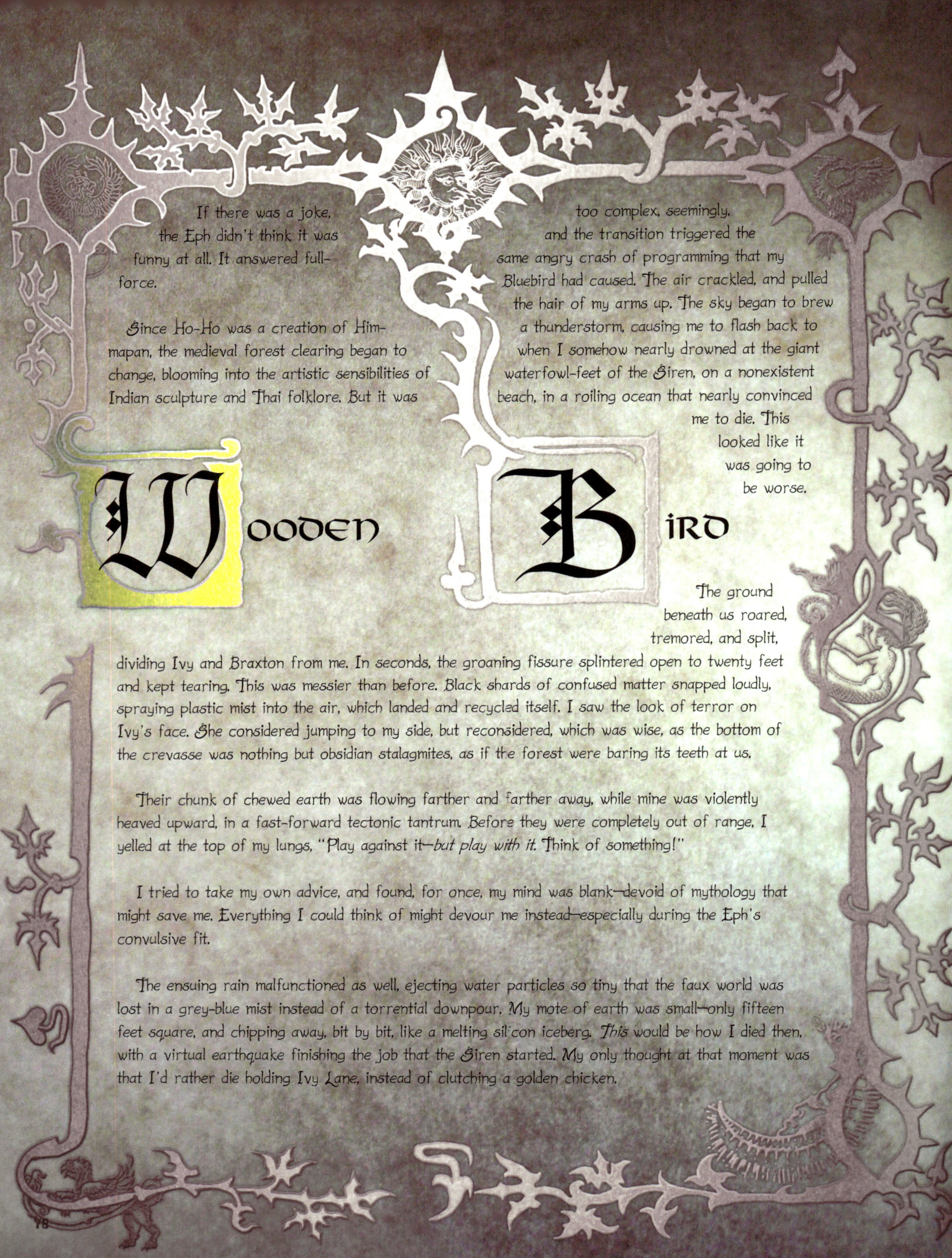

If there was a joke, the Eph didn't think it was funny at all. It answered full-force.

Since Ho-Ho was a creation of Himmapan, the medieval forest clearing began to change, blooming into the artistic sensibilities of Indian sculpture and Thai folklore. But it was too complex, seemingly, and the transition triggered the same angry crash of programming that my Bluebird had caused. The air crackled, and pulled the hair of my arms up. The sky began to brew a thunderstorm, causing me to flash back to when I somehow nearly drowned at the giant waterfowl-feet of the Siren, on a nonexistent beach, in a roiling ocean that nearly convinced me to die. This looked like it was going to be worse.

Wooden Bird

The ground beneath us roared, tremored, and split, dividing Ivy and Braxton from me. In seconds, the groaning fissure splintered open to twenty feet and kept tearing. This was messier than before. Black shards of confused matter snapped loudly, spraying plastic mist into the air, which landed and recycled itself. I saw the look of terror on Ivy's face. She considered jumping to my side, but reconsidered, which was wise, as the bottom of the crevasse was nothing but obsidian stalagmites, as if the forest were baring its teeth at us.

Their chunk of chewed earth was flowing farther and farther away, while mine was violently heaved upward, in a fast-forward tectonic tantrum. Before they were completely out of range, I yelled at the top of my lungs, "Play against it—*but play with it.* Think of something!"

I tried to take my own advice, and found, for once, my mind was blank—devoid of mythology that might save me. Everything I could think of might devour me instead—especially during the Eph's convulsive fit.

The ensuing rain malfunctioned as well, ejecting water particles so tiny that the faux world was lost in a grey-blue mist instead of a torrential downpour. My mote of earth was small—only fifteen feet square, and chipping away, bit by bit, like a melting silicon iceberg. *This* would be how I died then, with a virtual earthquake finishing the job that the Siren started. My only thought at that moment was that I'd rather die holding Ivy Lane, instead of clutching a golden chicken.

Suddenly, the thick mists parted. Two halves of smoky blue air were pulled asunder, like drawn curtains—tugged by the beak of a huge wooden bird!

The next thing I knew, I was aboard the bird, whose wooden clockwork gears and cogs turned to force wooden wings to flap. The function didn't match the form, but we were able to glide away from the disastrous glitch nonetheless. Ivy seemed to pick up on my disbelief, and Braxton gave me a distinct, terrified *"please let's not question this"* look.

She managed to grin, "The ancient Chinese swore that Lu Pan's Wooden Bird was the world's first true aircraft. Who are we to judge?"

"Handsomely done, Lane," I remarked. "That was clever, choosing a bird that was vague in history—and most importantly, not alive!"

I could hear Ivy whispering, repeating something under her breath, but by the time I understood her mantra, *"Don't say it...Don't say it,"* it was too late. I said exactly what she was afraid I would say—something I should have known better not to dare the Eph with—my absent-minded comment, *"Lu Pan's Wooden Bird was probably just a big kite, but dash it all—here we are!"*

As Ivy had already guessed, the walls, the sky and the air, *all had ears*...and the ground, too, which we were about to meet. Our spiteful, malcontent and malfunctioning host took the opportunity to downgrade our sky chariot into a something more akin to a flimsy kite and we went into a nose-dive.

Luckily, we had already been slowly descending, and the tumble was not too deadly. No matter how much we seemed to escape the blue fog, there was nowhere left inside the vast chamber that had not been affected by the corrupted landscape.

It looked like the result of a world war and a volcanic eruption. The ground was gritty and bare, interrupted only by glassy upheavals and ugly, unfinished terrain. Here a stone that looks like half a stone, and half black glass...there a hill that abruptly ends in a ninety degree slice. The angles were all wrong. There was nothing "of nature" about it anymore and it was disconcerting to the eyes.

The doctor seemed to shatter along with the scenery. First he had refused to get out of the broken Wooden Bird, and then he promptly vomited over the side. He was beleaguered, and began a litany of outrage and accusations that Ivy only stifled by warning that "the broken Eph was still listening," and..."Did he really want a militant variant to pick up on us fighting?!"

That did it. But he insisted that we decide on a new, last-ditch plan right then and there.

I asked him about something I had only then remembered. "What of the black spinning orb, that hovered and seemed to start up the entire simulation? Is it possible to summon it to us, and tamper with it?"

"The Command Orb? You don't have to summon it. It's here somewhere now, around us...just as cloaked as the damned door out of here. Randomly breaking it might mean anything from it turning that fog into sulfuric acid, to filling the entire chamber with water. And there's no way to interface with a Command Orb without the proper toolset. You usually need an actual keyed wire to get into it. It's old-school, on purpose. Only top technicians were qualified to work on real Ephs like this. But, as a last-ditch effort, that's not too bad. My plan is—"

"WAIT," Ivy interrupted. "The Ephemeral Artery is listening and responding. Doesn't that tell you that we can't announce any sort of plan out loud?"

"Alright then," I said, and, thinking I might throw the Eph for a loop, I pulled out a coin from my pocket and made to flip it. "I'll take heads, and whoever wins directs our next move."

I flipped the silver quarter into the air, but Ivy caught it, and hissed at me, "And why would *YOU* think that bifurcating our actions into two possibilities is the right thing to do?! The Eph might actually latch onto the idea that *one* of the two outcomes should *really be a downside*—as in, we would die, horribly."

It was then that I realized that Ivy was also breaking. Not by rage, but by the constant effort to stay one step ahead of an omnipotent mother-brain. For all I knew, I was also long since broken. We were severely dehydrated and hungry, as Ivy and I refused to eat or drink inside the simulation, citing the ill effects of consumables possibly reverting to slivers of base matter. Braxton, on the other hand, had reveled in it, even conjuring hot food at one point, and drinking enough water for all three of us. He always laughed at our refusal, but the whole thing reminded me of the old tales of fairy dimensions, wherein, eating fey food and partaking of their drink was the nail in your coffin, *always.*

She opened her hand and frowned at the silver coin. We all leaned in to look. "What is it, anyway?" she asked.

"A 1914 Barber Quarter," Braxton proudly announced. "That's my next love, after Ephemerals. What in the hell are you doing with a coin that old? And anyway, it's tails! So I'll tell you what we're gonna do." His eyes were wild, with roving whites as if he were in *REM* sleep while awake. He was going mad.

"We're gonna conjure explosives, and systematically BLOW SO MUCH OF THIS DAMNED ABOMINATION AWAY that it won't be able to repair itself before we uncover a door!"

He knocked the silver quarter from Ivy's outstretched palm, and laughed maniacally, but the quarter never stopped tinkling in the gloom. Soon we were watching the coin instead of him, as it was rolling up a cliff, and growing steadily larger.

By the time it came to rest at the crest of the crumpled hill, it was the size of a two-story house. The silvery heraldic eagle loomed over us, implacable and ominous. It's embossed edges were strangely pointed and sharp at this size and dimension.

"Wait a moment," I said, dumbfounded and pointing at the immense quarter, "We all emptied our pockets when we came in."

That comment was ignored. I could see Ivy's cogs turning on the symbolism that towered above us. "I know it's just an old coin, scaled up, but I'm trying to remember everything about the 'US eagle,'" she muttered to herself, transfixed, "But I'm too terrified to think."

Braxton's agitation had been instantly calmed by this surprising emanation from the Eph. He answered, without turning his gaze from the shimmering silver monolith, "It's

The Berunda

based on the great seal, and the national bird, the indigenous bald eagle...but it goes much further back than that. In the minds of the engravers of US coins, there was always a tendency toward Roman symbols. Beyond that, it's clutching an olive branch with 13 olives for peace, and in its other foot there are 13 arrows for war. Do you think what you said about bifurcated fate is really part of this?"

I was eager to add something—too eager, as always, "There are thousands of pages written on the eagle in heraldry, alone. Rome indeed had their 'Aquila' silver eagle, as written by Pliny the Elder. But so did Egypt, Persia, Germany, and many others throughout time. The eagle is on par with the lion as a king of beasts. Early on, some nations found a way to make their bird of war *more* fearsome, by giving it two heads instead of one. In fact, the eagle on US coinage is usually spread. The term "spread eagle" refers to an eagle with two heads. From there, we might mention another facet of its roots, Ganda Berunda, the monster who emanated from the wrath of Vishnu to threaten the entire Hindu pantheon—no easy feat! We're talking about millions of gods."

Embarrassed by running at the mouth, I added, "The reverse of the seal is 'The Eye of Providence,' which, if this Eph is, in some ways, 'thinking' on its own, then I'm surprised the watchful eye isn't its chosen symbol in all things."

When confronted as its own entity, the Ephemeral Artery seems only to feign an ability for the nuances of abstract symbolism, and instead expresses something obvious and threatening. The huge silver bird trumped our speculations in vexillology by peeling itself from the surface of the coin and simply coming to life. Worse, as if the Eph bore the mutable, flitting imagination of an impatient child, it began a shimmering transformation. Being the war bird of one hundred nations was not enough. With feigned strain, the eagle's head divided into two. It stretched, and shook out its plumage. The monster fixed four sharp eyes upon us and awaited our reaction. I imagine, grimly, that what this Eph sought, was to again feel revered in the face of its recent calamity. It would restore the status quo of our constant, collective terror.

Braxton, still moving and speaking as though in a daze, muttered, "Let's find out how much this Eph *is* thinking."

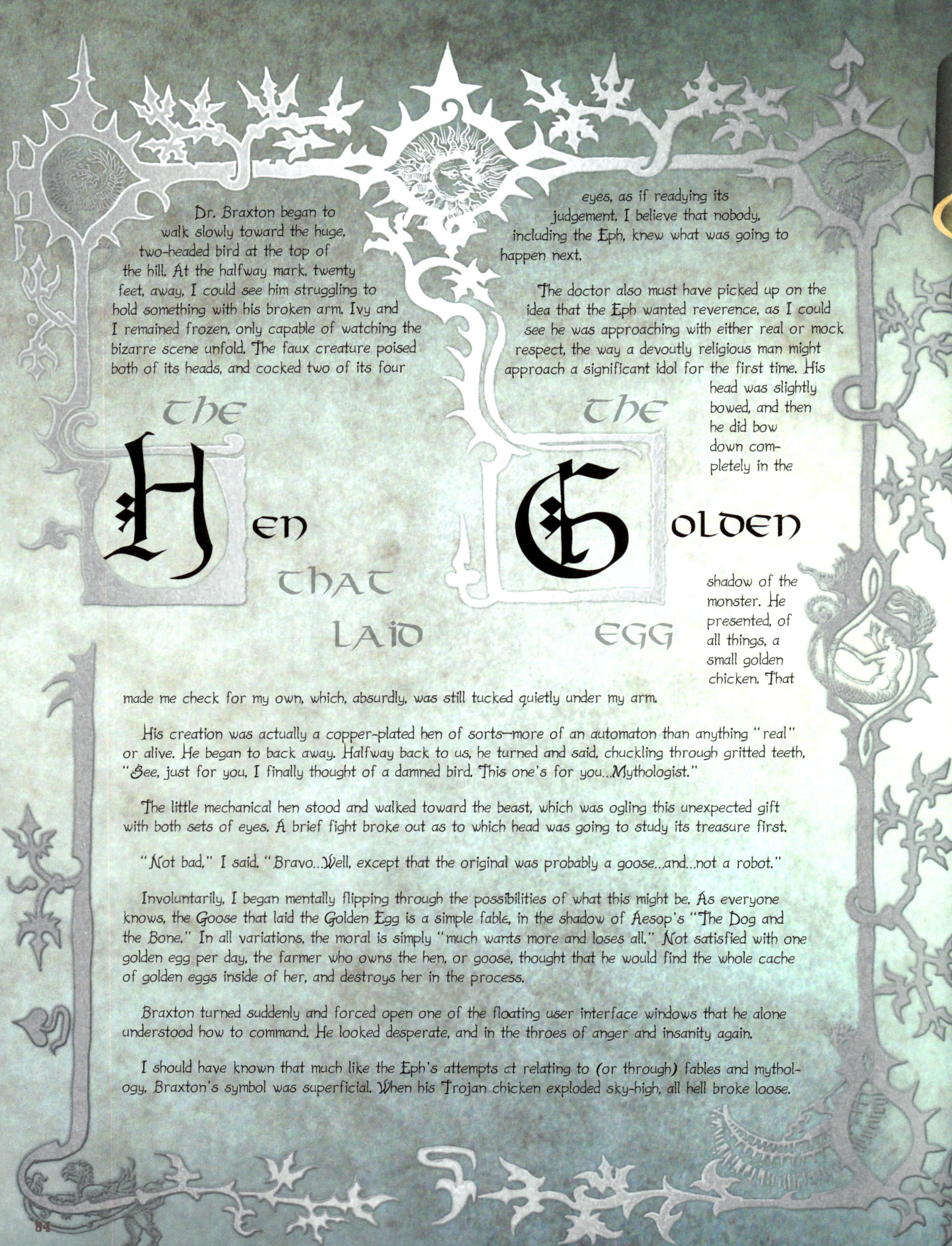

Dr. Braxton began to walk slowly toward the huge, two-headed bird at the top of the hill. At the halfway mark, twenty feet, away, I could see him struggling to hold something with his broken arm. Ivy and I remained frozen, only capable of watching the bizarre scene unfold. The faux creature poised both of its heads, and cocked two of its four eyes, as if readying its judgement. I believe that nobody, including the Eph, knew what was going to happen next.

The doctor also must have picked up on the idea that the Eph wanted reverence, as I could see he was approaching with either real or mock respect, the way a devoutly religious man might approach a significant idol for the first time. His head was slightly bowed, and then he did bow down completely in the

The Hen that Laid the Golden Egg

shadow of the monster. He presented, of all things, a small golden chicken. That made me check for my own, which, absurdly, was still tucked quietly under my arm.

His creation was actually a copper-plated hen of sorts—more of an automaton than anything "real" or alive. He began to back away. Halfway back to us, he turned and said, chuckling through gritted teeth, "See, just for you, I finally thought of a damned bird. This one's for you...Mythologist."

The little mechanical hen stood and walked toward the beast, which was ogling this unexpected gift with both sets of eyes. A brief fight broke out as to which head was going to study its treasure first.

"Not bad," I said. "Bravo...Well, except that the original was probably a goose...and...not a robot."

Involuntarily, I began mentally flipping through the possibilities of what this might be. As everyone knows, the Goose that laid the Golden Egg is a simple fable, in the shadow of Aesop's "The Dog and the Bone." In all variations, the moral is simply "much wants more and loses all." Not satisfied with one golden egg per day, the farmer who owns the hen, or goose, thought that he would find the whole cache of golden eggs inside of her, and destroys her in the process.

Braxton turned suddenly and forced open one of the floating user interface windows that he alone understood how to command. He looked desperate, and in the throes of anger and insanity again.

I should have known that much like the Eph's attempts at relating to (or through) fables and mythology, Braxton's symbol was superficial. When his Trojan chicken exploded sky-high, all hell broke loose.

BA-
BOOM!

Things began to spiral out of control from then on.

The explosion blew the rightmost head clean off at the shoulder, and knocked the Berunda, who was still partially three-dimensional, and partially flattened to its silver coin, over the cliff.

Braxton was busily typing into the portal, and amazingly, the black, revolving Command Orb appeared out of nowhere from above and was being pulled, as if against its own will, down toward the doctor. It came to rest only inches from him, but as he turned to work with it, the smoldering, monstrous bird breached the rim of the splintered gorge and roared, flapping wings that were now entirely free of the coin. As the heavy silver quarter slipped away, I saw its spangle of stars being sucked into its mouth. When it spied Dr. Braxton, it spit those stars as a crackling turbulent cone of energy.

When the beam touched the doctor, he was utterly disintegrated. He never had time to look up and see it coming. If he had been able to study it, I believe he might have been

9-headed Phoenix

astounded at the possibilities. I lament to think of all his theories on the matter. Was it merely a weaponized reconfiguration of the same mechanism the Eph uses to destroy and recycle its own matter? Or could it be a true death ray, in the simplest terms? Was it something that was uniquely concocted by a spiteful artificial intelligence once, never to be repeated, or studied, or understood, ever again?

Except that it was repeated a few times. When Ivy and I dodged in separate directions to tumble behind hunks of unfinished black boulders, I realized my left boot was smoldering and my pinky toe had been sheered off so cleanly, it was as if my foot was made of plastic. There was no blood and if there was pain, I couldn't feel it in the wake of adrenaline. I was more afraid for Ivy. She had tumbled safely but was looking at me, mouthing something, angrily. After the crackling buzz of Berunda's blast ceased, I could hear her yelling, "WHY ARE YOU STILL CARRYING THAT INFERNAL CHICKEN?!"

It was true. I had been walking, planning, gesturing, lecturing about heraldic eagles, and now doing acrobatics, all while clutching my pet celestial chicken, Ho-Ho. My little luck talisman was looking worse for wear. In desperation, I made a child's leap of faith and commanded my Chicken of Luck to fly forth in mortal combat! As I peered over the top of my boulder, I saw that the monster had become entirely a thing of its Hindu story and instead of an olive branch, now held a war elephant in its talons, which it loosed upon us like a homing missile.

The elephant juggernaut charged over the terrain, obliterating my boulder and shattering itself to black dust in the effort. I was thrown to the edge of the cliff, where I held on for my life.

I tried to think clearly amidst the tumult. This wasn't the first time that day that I could taste my imminent demise. I was getting used to the idea. It occurred to me, then, that we might be able to turn a flailing, breaking Eph against itself.

I tried a willful command toward my little golden chicken, which was doing its best to flap about in the face of the snapping eagle. "You will be reborn a Phoenix. You are Jui Feng, and Fenghuang, the nine-headed emperor over all birds. You will force this demon to supplicate."

Running from her cover over to the edge of the cliff, Ivy pulled me up. In her trail was the Berunda's death ray, narrowly missing her, but winging the confused Command Orb, which was still spinning where Dr. Braxton once stood. A section of the orb went the way of my toe—disintegrated—as was my Chicken of Luck.

Yet, phoenix birds are synonymous with resurrection. I don't know if it was the damage to the orb, or the luck factor of my chicken, but from the ashes of Ho-Ho rose a superior for Berunda—a flying, nine-headed behemoth!

The breath of the Berunda disintegrated two of the heads of the Nine-Headed Phoenix, but the Chinese bird god soon won out, as its six heads swarmed over its body and tore it to pieces.

By order of events, the Eph had been trumped by itself, which seemed to give it pause. The grandiose Phoenix simply flapped away into the horizon, illuminated by the continually flashing purple lightning that had persisted since the Eph had botched its thunderstorm.

For Dr. Braxton, Ivy and I exchanged a look of earnest sorrow (no matter how difficult he had been at times). Admittedly, we were also left with the fretful fear of losing our one true expert on Ephemeral Arteries. Maybe there was no hope of getting out?

We followed the gliding dark spot fearfully, and sure enough, it made for a return swoop, for which there was not much we could do in anticipation.

After all that I'd seen, I thought I had become inured to the wonder and the spectacle that the Eph was capable of. It was akin to being trapped

Thunderbird

in a forty-hour magician's show where the magic loses its luster after the first few tricks. Yet I was wrong in that assumption—perhaps the most wrong, of any of my ill-conceived notions about its workings.

I instantly recognized the shadow that swept over us. It was no longer Chinese but Native American. It was a bird of lore simultaneously of infamous distinction and yet completely open to interpretation.

As the Thunderbird swept over us, we were absolutely torrented in rain that seemed to emanate from between its wooden, totem-esque feathers.

"Why?!" I said, shrugging at Ivy.

"It's a vengeful bird of storms. It's a bird of many names and faces. It has at least a dozen names in the histories of Pacific Northwest tribes alone. It is what the Eph wants it to be," Ivy answered. "Like everything else it throws at us."

"The one thunderbird was said to live at the peak of a mountain, a servitor of The Great Spirit. That's the one that controls rain," I concluded. "The Sioux said they were guardians against their antagonists in the oral traditions—the serpentine Unktehila. But, you're right. It just keeps dumping rain on us. Look at how fast the ruined ground is puddling up. Does it mean to wash us away? Has it reasoned that *we are pollutants*? Its very own computer virus?" I posited.

"What would the doctor say? By my time, some people had written that an advanced Ephemeral without users might be like an idle, frustrated mind gone insane. There's just too much...at the ready," Ivy said.

But I had worked out its true purpose by simply looking at the flooding ground beneath us. There, in one of the deep furrows caused by the death ray of Gandaberunda, was a door in the floor, much like an industrial hatchway.

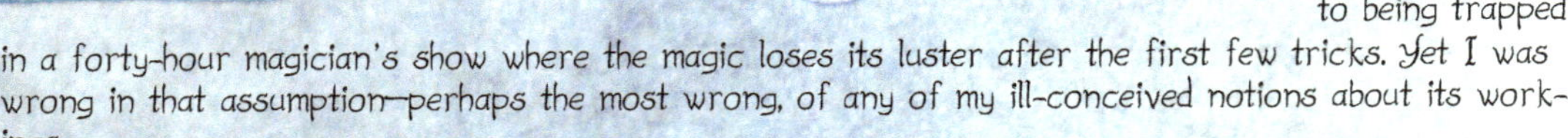

TOUR THREE:
THE BIRDS OF WONDERLAND
A DARING ESCAPE FROM THE EPHEMERAL ARTERY

Dodo

"I think it was trying to cover up the door. In that case, it's too wounded to recycle around us. We *did* manage to break it...if only a little," I said, with renewed hope.

"Well, we can credit the doctor, and honor him when we're out," Ivy answered.

We opened it with great difficulty and tossed some loose splinters of the black matter down the hole and listened, as best we could, over the downpour. It sounded like it was about a twelve foot drop. I made to jump in first, saying, "Once more, through the rabbit hole," as my epitaph, in case I was jumping to my doom, but Ivy caught me, and showed me that there were ladder rungs, after all.

At the bottom, I accidentally put the foot with my severed toe down first, and winced. Now, there was pain. My bare, cauterized skin touched cold tile flooring below, much like the floor in the hallway on the way into the abandoned complex.

Soft, LED overhead lights automatically came on three seconds after we had entered, which was customary for that time.

"We're out, 'M'...We're really out! We beat it!" Ivy was ecstatic.

"What is this?" I asked. "Some kind of control wing?"

"I have no idea," Ivy said. "Remember, in my time Ephs are like video games for kids. They are nothing...*nothing* like this anymore."

It looked more like a work-a-day snack room than anything. There were vending machines still stocked with snack packs of cheese crackers. There were those brands that always seem to endure the test of time—rolls of wintergreen candies and bags of hard pretzels, dipped in carob, since chocolate had not yet been successfully resurrected in the 2340's (cocoa, much like coffee, regrettably, would never be quite right again).

Alas, we had no way to work them. Thirsty and starving, we added vandalism and petty theft, to breaking and entering, bashing open as much as we could so we could finally eat and drink.

Overhead, we could still hear the patter of heavy rain, reverberating. There was enough water running down through the hatch that I climbed back up to shut the trap door, but not before I was startled by a small brown, waterlogged mouse, who came tumbling down the chute. "Oh, the horrors you must have seen, little mouse," I said. "Wise move, bailing on your warehouse of monsters."

With our humble feast spread over the table, we said very little. The air was alive with the sounds of crumpling cellophane and the popping of plastic containers of carbonated colas and juices.

Ivy shed a single, heavy tear for the doctor. I dried it with my sleeve and put my hand on hers for a moment, but no words could express our tangled emotions. I imagine she has, and always will have, a deep-set resentment for the way I pulled her and others into my orbit.

"Much wants more and loses all," I thought. That was either Dr. Braxton's last laugh at me, or his wisest of all scientific observations...of me.

Exhausted, we exited the snack room, and walked slowly down the hall, me dragging my tingling, newly deformed foot.

The lights in the hallway kicked on in the same way, but in a cascading stream of glowing white that meandered away from us, where it abruptly ended about eighty feet down. There were eight doors, four on either side, spaced equally apart.

"This is definitely the control wing. One of these doors has to lead to real, live sunlight. I can't wait," I said, sighing.

"Well, let's just start with the ones that are unlocked," Ivy said, as she was already trying the first door. It opened easily, but she looked into the room, and turned back before I could see past her shoulders, muttering, "No...No. No—this isn't happening."

I peered in, my heart in my throat, wondering wildly if perhaps the team that ran this complex had committed suicide—all hung themselves, and somehow, their funding corporation, or the military, just hadn't found them yet. It was a real suspicion in my mind. In that case, we'd better hurry before we might be implicated in such a grim affair. The truth was far stranger, and worse.

We had interrupted a bizarre confabulation of animals, busily arguing over something. In the forefront, was a Dodo, flanked on all sides by lorries, ducks, eaglets and several other curious creatures. A girl of about eight, sat on a thimble beside them, waiting for their argument to subside, looking wistfully into the distance. None of these creatures was over two feet tall, including the little girl. There were common objects surrounding them that were

CONSUL
THE
EDUCATED
MONKEY

of equally disproportionate sizes, mostly made up of 19th century sewing utensils. Though the cavalcade of animals looked up at us, staring creepily with their cursed anthropomorphic grins and semi-human expressions, the little girl took no notice whatsoever. "No prizes left for you, sir," was all that the portly, extinct bird had time to say to me, before I closed the door in shock.

Ivy was already back in the snack room pacing, and repeating things under her breath, as was her custom during strain. "We're not out. We never left. It won't let us leave. We're gonna march around in this madness until we're dead. We'll be found years later as skeletons who either died holding one another, or with our hands around each other's throats, BECAUSE I'M ALREADY LOSING MY MIND!" Look at this—do you see this? Please tell me you do."

"I do." I said, adjusting my voice carefully to the most delicate cadence I possessed. There on the table, where there should have been a cluster of empty plastic containers, sticky with our stale sugary backwash, were now nothing but glass bottles with the crystalline etching and embossed labeling of a bygone era. Tied around each rim was an over-sized paper tag with the handwritten phrase "Drink Me" in lavish English script. The food wrappers were replaced by the crumbs of cakes dotted by currants and tiny cinnamon heart candies that spelled out fragments of the words "Eat Me."

And we had. We had finally violated the one rule that Ivy and I had instinctually and stubbornly adhered to inside the Eph. In the name of one thousand fabled warnings in fifty varying cultures and at least twenty languages: "When one finds themselves inside a fairy tale, do not eat their food, nor drink their drink." Once the hapless protagonist had partaken of their strange host's food, they seemed to have some sort of power over them.

"The little mouse," was all I managed to eek out, sounding like a mouse myself. "That's when it happened. We left the hatch open long enough for the Command Orb to hover down here, and it covered itself in the illusion of a small mouse escaping the flooding rain above."

"And for some reason, it launched into full-on Wonderland? That's what Ephs are used for in my time—mostly as a way to get history and decent literature into kids," Ivy said, throwing up her arms.

"You saw how the damage we did affected things up there. It was already in fits and starts—seeming to break down of its own accord. Don't despair yet, Miss Lane. This is a different barrel of monkeys—well, same monkeys, different barrel."

"If you remember," I continued, "I made that comment about going 'down the rabbit hole,' and when the Eph snuck down here with us, it latched onto that comment, because it was forced to change channels, from its murderous rampage upstairs, to the story book of my quote. I believe that means we really are in a regular room, at least partially. Look around—there's no sign of the ailing Eph's atomic disintegration in the floor or walls. It's all a little too perfect, right? Remember why the immersive network was dubbed an 'Ephemeral Artery' in the first place. 'Ephemeral,' because of the tendency of the human mind to conjure a sentimental jumble of memories—much like mental scrapbooking, and 'Arterial' because of the technology that eventually allowed the pliable wiring to grow and flow into any available space, so home users could move from room to room. Don't you see, Lane? We ARE out. It's just keeping us in the shared mental hallucination—no more programmable matter down here—this is all just in our minds!"

"OK," Ivy said, slowly, "So, how do we break the looking glass this time?"

"All we have to do is keep our heads screwed on a little bit longer. We can't let the Eph convince us of anything danger- ous. We'll just search until we find the actual exit that leads us beyond its reach," I suggested.

Just then I thought of my run-in with the Alkonost and the Siren, and what became of poor Cale Corbett, and I realized I'd never really been sure how I broke that illusion. I had carried with me the conceit that I'd overpowered it with my mental prowess for mythology. Finally! My branch of knowledge had become a mighty weapon to triumph against high technology. Now that I faced the same challenge, I felt completely uncertain as to what truly happened that night.

I decided not to tell Ivy Lane about the twitchy part, where we almost "drowned" to death inside our own imaginations. She had been through too much already. Maybe we would be spared another violent attack. Perhaps we had broken enough

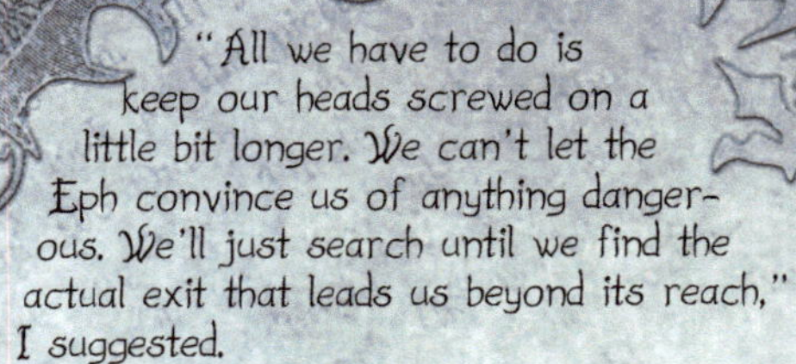

Gryphon

of this Eph's brain that it might have forgotten how to be wily in the name of total domination over its users.

"Let's keep it light, Lane." I said, in the best casual tone I could muster. This time, I opened the first door on the left (as the Dodo's room had no discernible exit). "I totally expect to see the Gryphon, from *Alice In Wonderland*, Chapter IX...or X, I think."

And so it was that Alice was being whisked away to court to become part of the jury in the "Trial of the Stolen Tarts." The Gryphon took Alice gently by the hand, and pulled her up onto its back to rush through a maze made of ivy-coated hedges and white stone paths.

Most every character in Wonderland seemed to have a parallel in Lewis Carroll's life or times. The Dodo was Carroll himself, aka Charles Dodgson, written as a self-parody of his stammering ("Do-Do-Do-Dodgson"). The Gryphon was a pompous and dismissive erudite adult presence (one of many) beset to confound Alice.

Part eagle and part lion, ancient gryphons seemed to be one of the first and most prevalent chimeric mascots. The Greeks were gryphon-crazy, adding their talons to as many columns as they could. It's pos- sible that they found the fossilized remains of Ceratopsian dinosaurs which, igniting their imaginations, came through as gryphons in their sculpture.

In medieval bestiaries, gryphons took on further dimension, cited as mating for life. If ground and brewed, their claws and feathers might restore sight to the blind. Churches used the gryphon in heraldry to symbolize the finality of marriage.

I was afraid to mention to Ivy that, after all we had been through, I was still getting a tiny thrill out of seeing the birds I had hoped to see. I decided to blame it entirely on the Eph.

"Notice," I said, in mock-ponderance, "How it's still mostly showing us birds as some sort of carry-over from upstairs...'Curiouser, and curiouser.'"

Ivy shot me a dubious look.

Despite that in our minds, the room appeared as a labyrinthine garden, the actual space was a dead end. It was an ivy-strewn maze devoid of any real choices. Without further discussion, we crisscrossed to the next room, but we found that it wasn't a real door at all and we were met with only the painted cement blocks behind it.

Just to be sure it wasn't a trick, I attempted to walk through them, with comic result.

The next room adjoined to its neighbor, and therefore afforded the Eph space that it lapped up hungrily, attempting to paint a vast, illusory woodland inside. Was this the Tulgey Wood from Carroll's second book, "Through the Looking Glass?" The paper landscape was rendered from old etchings and pen-and-ink illustrations from throughout classic literature. Here, the Wonderland theme was bleeding off the margins, as we discerned creatures from hundreds of different books, stalking the paths like feral wildlife.

The element of danger resumed in this room. I could sense it in the sick orange and green

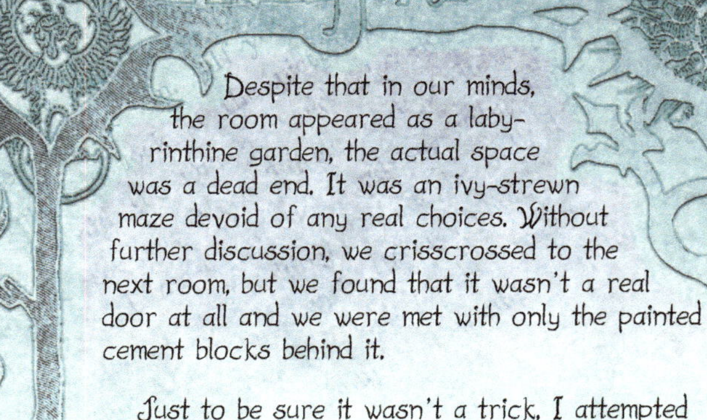

Jub Jub Bird

light that seeped through the ink-blotted canopy. The air took on the moldering smell of old money and dirty coins. These were the hallmarks of a calm before a storm, and I thought I heard the sound of distant thunder once again, but it was the rumbling thrum of a dragonlike beast smashing through the woods, knocking down paper trees making impact tremors. It was so titanic, it did not notice us beneath its tree-trunk legs, as it crossed over the path in one stride. For a split-second, I saw its head, an amalgamation of Rhinoceros Beetle and dragon, making unintelligible squelching grunts. I knew what the Eph was using to twist its picture book forest into something foreboding. It was the king of all nonsensical monstrosities. Carroll's ponderous lyrics played involuntarily in my mind:

> Twas brillig, and the slithy toves
> Did gyre and gimble in the wabe:
> All mimsy were the borogoves,
> And the mome raths outgrabe.

> "Beware the Jabberwock, my son!
> The jaws that bite, the claws that catch!
> Beware the Jubjub bird, and shun
> The frumious—"

I had barely taken notice of her in my peripheral, kneeling at the foot of what could only be a Tumtum Tree, slowly approaching a beautiful butterfly with her finger set to be its perch. Just as she reached out, to touch its delicate paper wings, I screamed, "Ivy, *STOP RIGHT THERE!*" and luckily she did. The butterfly seemed to turn inside out, and became a thing between a bird and a scorpion, all feathers and stingers.

We had felt lucky in avoiding the towering Jabberwocky but that was only a distraction, meant to keep us off guard for the rest of the poem's denizens. It was a ruse!

She backed away from the Eph's version of the Jubjub bird, and we kept our wits close at hand from then on.

Was the Eph losing its focus? Other tales and books continued to hemorrhage in. A dash of Lyman Frank Baum's *Wizard of Oz* sprinkled over our trail, beginning with the fragments of gilded yellow bricks.

The glimpse of a Flying Monkey horrified Ivy, as she claimed to have always feared them from her very first viewing of the ancient film, still shown in her time as tradition.

I had hoped this was a further sign that the Eph was bleeding from the wounds caused by the snicker-snack of Dr. Braxton's "vorpal hen," and its explosion so near the Command Orb. Somewhere above us, unseen, it revolved still—its head full of lasers and quantum calculations. It would keeping spinning its yarns at us like a frantic spider who is watching flies break free of its web.

The tight grouping of trees pushed us back and forth along the path, unable to convince our own minds otherwise. I guessed that the trees were taking the place of desks and real-world obstacles that might cause us to stumble or

Ibong Adarna

twist an ankle. There was a gamble in ignoring its barriers. To reach out and touch them proves nothing. The Eph simply convinces you they are solid, even if they are not.

Ahead, there was a clearing scratched out in pieces of old money, mostly consisting of U.S. one-dollar bills. The thirteen-step pyramid was in ruin, choked by monetary vines and leaves, with its all-seeing Eye of Providence toppled away. I had just enough time to wonder if this was the Eph's way of conceding defeat, when a bird of considerable splendor flew by us. Though it held the olive branch of peace, plucked from the symbology of the theme of currency, I knew better—that this spectacle, like the venomous Jubjub Bird, was a ruse. When the creature let loose its bird song, I was sure this was an attempt of the Eph to use a last-ditch arrow from its quiver.

The song of the bird was immediately hypnotic, masked by beautiful Spanish melodies and music. That was the give-away. I remembered the Ibong Adarna, a magical bird from the epic poem "Corrido at Buhay na Pinagdaanan nang Tatlong Principeng anak nang Haring Fernando at nang Reina Valeriana sa Cahariang Berbania" to which the long title explains, is about the exploits of three princes, the chief hero among them being Don Juan.

At the start of the tale, both of Don Juan's brothers fail to capture the Ibong Adarna, the most rare and mystical of birds. The Adarna is able to sing seven melodies that lull them to sleep, after which, the bird unceremoniously hits them with its droppings and turns them to stone. I was uncertain what the Eph could do to simulate petrification, but it was probably within its power to fire neural oscillations at our brains, and induce sleep—especially when we were both so exhausted. The prospect was terrifying.

Again, my mind reeled for a defense. In the story, Don Juan sliced his palms once for each melody, and squeezed lime juice into the wounds so that he could avoid the drowsiness. I had neither blade nor citrus, so I started stamping my disintegrated toe into the ground to send waves of pain through my body.

The bird was too obscure for Ivy this time and she submitted to the effects of the music almost immediately. I had just enough strength to carry her over my shoulder toward a section of "forest" that was curiously like a hallway.

ᚷonstrous ℭrow

As I ran, I thought of the endings to both of Lewis Carroll's tales.

In Wonderland, Alice becomes both part of the jury and of those prosecuted for irrelevant mishaps. Just when she gets the upper hand over the supervising presence, she is judged and chastised. The playing card soldiers of the Queen of Hearts attack en masse, until she awakens from the pseudo-nightmare.

The Looking-Glass World was another dreamscape for improbable creatures, but it was also very much a live game of chess played between Red and White Queens, with Alice as a pawn. In the end, she is crowned a queen, and eventually takes the sleeping Red King in checkmate. As in Wonderland, gaining control over her surroundings means overstaying her welcome, and she is hurled out of the dream in the tumult of her victory feast coming to life.

Alice is never allowed to win, truly.

I was worried about Ivy, who seemed to be stricken by a feverish half-sleep. I moved her to my front, and did my best to carry her in both arms, looking down, saying, "How is it going to end? Are we going to be stabbed by a deck of cards, or crowned in a feast?"

Ivy looked so weakened, but in the throes of the fever, I heard her say, "Feast. We ate the food, and now we'll be here forever...There is no end."

"Ivy," I said as softly as I could, between gasps from carrying her, "We just ate real-world crackers. The Eph put a curtain over it, *after*. Just like there's a curtain over us, *but we're going to make it.*"

After that, she devolved into random quotes from both books, which were strangely cryptic.

As I breached the opening of what seemed like a hallway, my motion began to tug and drag at the contents of the room, as if the whole illusion were elastic and ready to fray apart at the seams. The

Artist's / Transcriber's Note ~ 1: There are myriad other creatures that the Mythologist describes from the diffusion phase of the Ephemeral Artery, including several creatures of Oz, and numerous emanations from films, video games and art throughout history.

effect was disorienting to say the least, and I smacked into a solid, office-esque wall for a second, which heartened me.

Above, two sides of the faux forest attempted to curl over the hall like scribbled, skeletal fingers but it snapped in the middle, and the collective ink of so many drawings seemed to bleed together, diffusing into a dark grey stain—another angry storm of sorts. From those darkened clouds of ink came another bird of Carroll's tales, the "end-bird," whose only role seemed to be to frighten his protagonist off the margin and into a new chapter. The briefly mentioned Monstrous Crow, a storm who left nothingness in its wake because it *was* nothingness.

I glimpsed it for one mere moment, flying overhead. It was the size of a jet plane, pieced together in a jigsaw of the rolled pages of books. It was true—in its wake, there was nothing, save for a few drifting pages, lost like loosened feathers from its massive, papery wings. I could finally see the hall for what it really was, and I opened a door to another set of rungs, and an emergency hatch in the ceiling.

Ivy had glimpsed the Monstrous Crow fly over, and wide-eyed, had begun muttering pieces of the conversation between Alice and the Tweedles when they had encountered the Red King sleeping,

" 'Why, you're only a sort of thing in his dream! If the King awakes, you go out—bang!—just like a candle!' "

I took her meaning, fevered or not, and tried to comfort her. "We're real, Ivy. I promise you, we are real, and if you climb these rungs, we will breathe real air again."

She did the best she could, but I had to climb behind her, and strain to hold her onto the ladder. Finally, I had no choice but to lock her arms over the final rungs, fling open the portal and climb over her.

"Take my hand!" I begged, drawing fresh, crisp air for the first time in at least fifty hours. But Ivy was so confused—muddled by the sleep attack. Her mind stretched far enough to snap apart, just like the Eph's forest.

"That's not how the Looking-Glass book ends," she said, despondent. "It ends with the Red King waking up, and we never know who dreamt who. We never know who dreamt who." She repeated this again and again, and then started to unfurl her arms, to let go and fall backward, into the hatch, to be lost forever to the Ephemeral Artery.

Time seemed to stop..."Much wants more and loses all."

Was that what the Gamayun was trying to tell me? Were those words the final judgement of Doctor Braxton? Would this be my Achilles' Heel, from now into eternity?

I grabbed her and pulled as hard as I could. When I was sure we were both outside, I remember blacking out. I am uncertain if that was from exhaustion, or from extracting ourselves from the dreamscape.

I looked down into the hatch, and I could see the damaged black Command Orb, hovering, making its sound of an angry hive of bees. The red pin lights of its true form had gathered to form something like a blinking eye, and I thought, for a moment, that it reminded me of a child, left on the playground with no toys and no companions.

But then it reached out for us, menacingly, in the only way that it could. I felt the light touch upon my arm and recoiled from the growing, translucent wiring that accommodates its tyrannical control over space.

I pulled us away from the growing plastic vine and watched as it withered back down in the natural, ultraviolet rays of sunlight. I kicked the hatch over it, letting the heavy hatch smack the orb back down, hard.

I had hoped Ivy would be instantly better. I held her in my arms, apologizing for the danger I put her in.

"When she finally opened her eyes, she looked up at me, and said, "Who...are you, though...really?"

I was stricken by the question. In all my recent encounters with man, beast and bird, no one had really pressed me for that. All I ever had to do was prove that I could travel time, and they always followed.

"I...can't remember. But I'm still 'M' for now...And your M, always."

She smiled weakly, and managed, "Well, we will have to do something about that, if we can. But tell me, M...Isn't it always going to haunt you, from here-on-out?...Think about it...How can we ever really know that we're out?"

End: Tour 1, but the
Mythologist will
forge on ahead, in:
Birds of Lore II

Bibliography:

(partial)

Carroll, Lewis, John Tenniel, and Martin Gardner. The Annotated Alice. New York [u.a.: Norton, 2000. Print.

Karnchanapayap, Yongkiat, Onuma Chintanasatit, and Vytot Upatising.
"Himmapan: The Mythical Creatures of the East." Himmapan: The Mythical Creatures of the East.
http://www.himmapan.com   Http://www.shopssquare.com/, n.d. Web. 17 Feb. 2013.

"Alkonost." Wikipedia. Wikimedia Foundation, 24 Mar. 2013. Web. 14 Sept. 2012.

"Konjaku Gazu Zoku Hyakki." Wikipedia. Wikimedia Foundation, 28 Feb. 2013. Web. 7 Mar. 2013.

Allan, Tony. The Mythic Bestiary: The Illustrated Guide to the World's Most Fantastical Creatures. London: Duncan Baird, 2008. Print.

Corey, Melinda, and George Ochoa. The Encyclopedia of the Victorian World: A Reader's Companion to the People, Places, Events, and Everyday Life of the Victorian Era. New York: Henry Holt and, 1996. Print.

Shuker, Karl, and Mark Chorvinsky. From Flying Toads to Snakes with Wings: From the Pages of Fate Magazine. St. Paul (Minnesota): Llewellyn, 1997. Print.

Grundy, Benjamin, Aaron Wright, and Elliot Birch. "Mysterious Universe." Mysterious Universe. 8th Kind Pty Ltd, 1 Jan. 2006. Web. 21 July 2012.

Manguel, Alberto, and Gianni Guadalupi. The Dictionary of Imaginary Places. New York: Harcourt Brace, 2000. Print.

Rose, Carol. Giants, Monsters, and Dragons: An Encyclopedia of Folklore, Legend, and Myth. Santa Barbara, CA: ABC-CLIO, 2000. Print.

Li, Sean. "Why Is a Raven Like a Writing Desk? | A Reasoner's Miscellany." A Reasoners Miscellany. Wordpress, n.d. Web. 24 July 2013.

Future ^Hopeful Volumes in the "Of Lore" series:

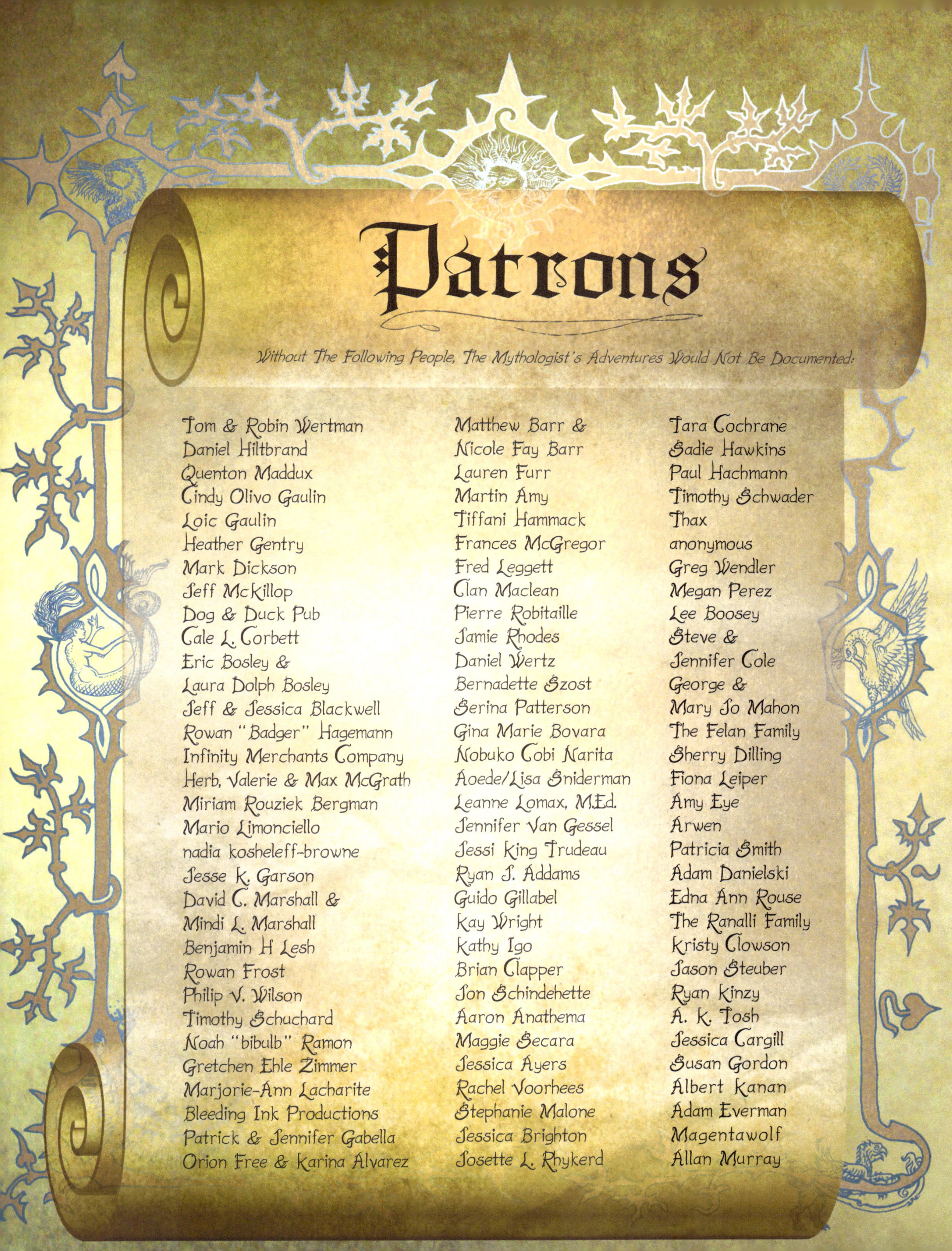

Patrons

Tom & Robin Wertman
Daniel Hiltbrand
Quenton Maddux
Cindy Olivo Gaulin
Loic Gaulin
Heather Gentry
Mark Dickson
Jeff McKillop
Dog & Duck Pub
Cale L. Corbett
Eric Bosley &
Laura Dolph Bosley
Jeff & Jessica Blackwell
Rowan "Badger" Hagemann
Infinity Merchants Company
Herb, Valerie & Max McGrath
Miriam Rouziek Bergman
Mario Limonciello
nadia kosheleff-browne
Jesse K. Garson
David C. Marshall &
Mindi L. Marshall
Benjamin H Lesh
Rowan Frost
Philip V. Wilson
Timothy Schuchard
Noah "bibulb" Ramon
Gretchen Ehle Zimmer
Marjorie-Ann Lacharite
Bleeding Ink Productions
Patrick & Jennifer Gabella
Orion Free & Karina Alvarez

Matthew Barr &
Nicole Fay Barr
Lauren Furr
Martin Amy
Tiffani Hammack
Frances McGregor
Fred Leggett
Clan Maclean
Pierre Robitaille
Jamie Rhodes
Daniel Wertz
Bernadette Szost
Serina Patterson
Gina Marie Bovara
Nobuko Cobi Narita
Aoede/Lisa Sniderman
Leanne Lomax, M.Ed.
Jennifer Van Gessel
Jessi King Trudeau
Ryan S. Addams
Guido Gillabel
Kay Wright
Kathy Igo
Brian Clapper
Jon Schindehette
Aaron Anathema
Maggie Secara
Jessica Ayers
Rachel Voorhees
Stephanie Malone
Jessica Brighton
Josette L. Rhykerd

Tara Cochrane
Sadie Hawkins
Paul Hachmann
Timothy Schwader
Thax
anonymous
Greg Wendler
Megan Perez
Lee Boosey
Steve &
Jennifer Cole
George &
Mary Jo Mahon
The Felan Family
Sherry Dilling
Fiona Leiper
Amy Eye
Arwen
Patricia Smith
Adam Danielski
Edna Ann Rouse
The Ranalli Family
Kristy Clowson
Jason Steuber
Ryan Kinzy
A. K. Tosh
Jessica Cargill
Susan Gordon
Albert Kanan
Adam Everman
Magentawolf
Allan Murray

In Acknowledgement:

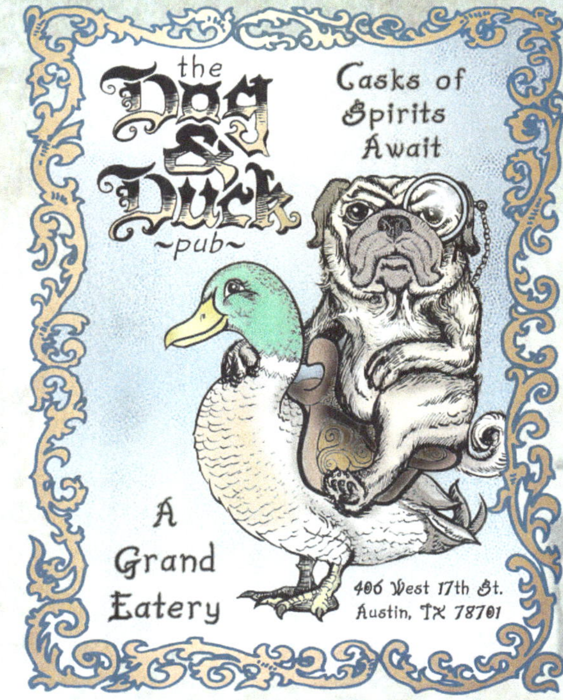

the
Dog
& Duck
~pub~
Casks of
Spirits
Await
A
Grand
Eatery
406 West 17th St.
Austin, TX 78701

Dr. Karl Shuker's
SHUKER
NATURE
ENCYCLOPAEDIA OF NEW
& REDISCOVERED ANIMALS

The Gentleman's Type Tool
~ for Windows & Mac ~
Type
"Type 3.2" font editor was used
to complete "Mythologist's Hand,"
the typeface of "Birds of Lore"
CR8 Software
Solutions Ltd.
3.2

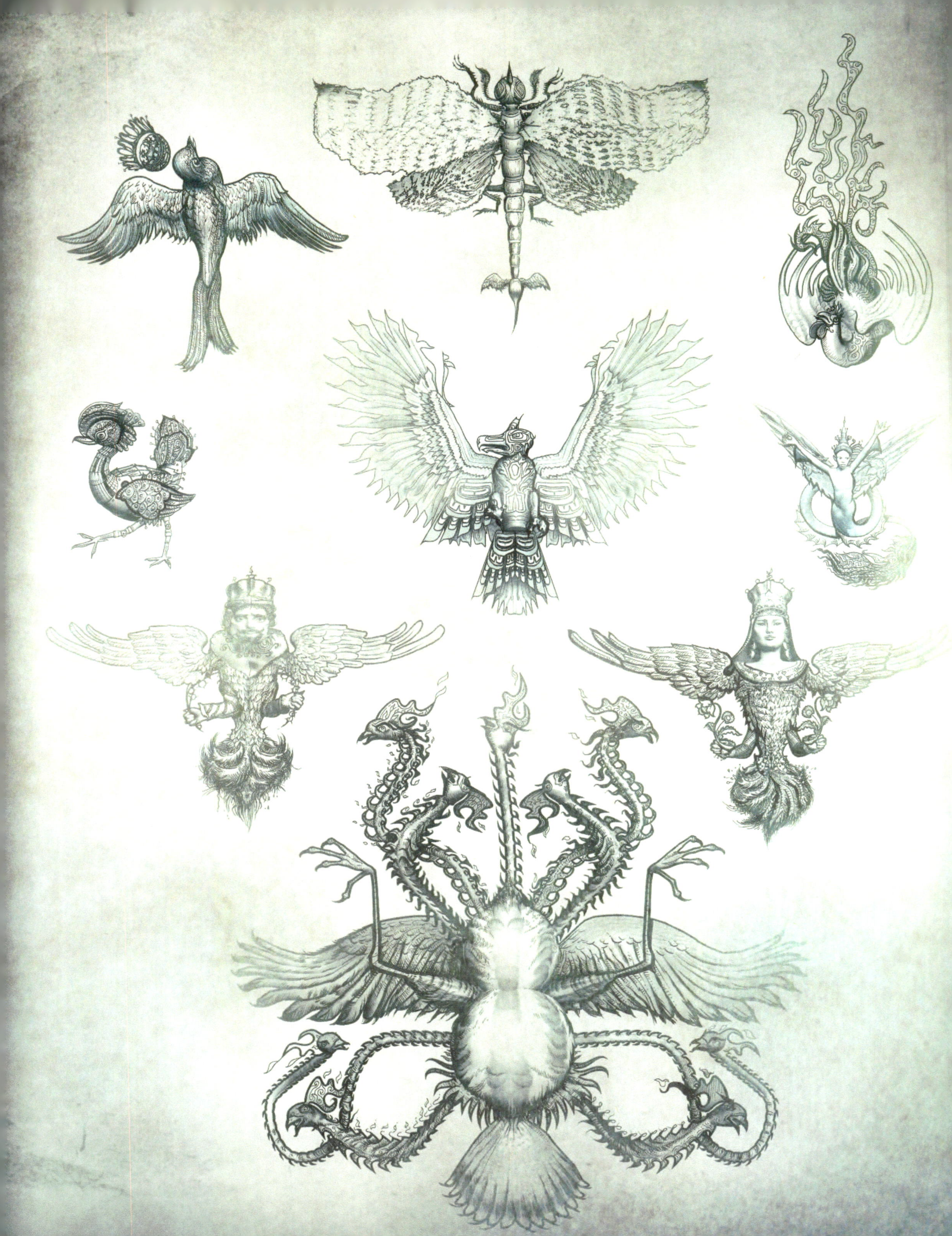